Sandra Chick

I Never Told Her I Loved Her

First published by The Women's Press Limited 1989
A member of the Namara Group
34 Great Sutton Street, London EC1V ODX

This is a work of fiction and any resemblance to actual
persons living or dead is purely coincidental.

British Library Cataloguing in Publication Data

Chick, Sandra
  I never told her I loved her.
  I. Title
  823'.914[F]

  ISBN 0–7043–4912–4

Typeset by MC Typeset Ltd, Gillingham, Kent

Printed and bound in Great Britain by Cox and Wyman,
Reading, Berks

With thanks to Robyn Slovo,
Carole Spedding and Nevil

Sandra Chick is the popular young author of *Push Me, Pull Me* (Livewire Books for Teenagers 1987), winner of *The Other Award* for Progressive Children's Literature, a Feminist Book Fortnight 1987 'Selected Twenty' title and short-listed for *The Observer* Teenage Fiction Prize 1987. She has also contributed to several short story anthologies. She lives in the West Country.

One

Dad's got old, suddenly.

I used to believe that everyone grew older little by little. Now I know, for some, the process is fast and harsh. The changes in him shock me, though I pretend I haven't noticed, so's not to make it worse by pushing it in his face.

Funny how I never noticed Mum changing. Well, I *did*, but I didn't see it as being permanent. She was poorly. When you're poorly you look different, when you recover you return to normal.

Dad was the one that told me, eventually, that she'd 'gone'. Gone where? Gone out? Gone mad? Gone but would soon be back? I wanted to ask – why don't you say she's *dead*? I wanted to cry, but couldn't. As far as I'm aware, he couldn't either.

Some people sent sympathy cards, we thanked them as if it was a birthday. Others asked if we needed help, we thanked them, but said we'd be fine. Some just decided to steer well clear until the awkward period was, by their judgment, over. It was as if having someone die was an embarrassment. Like taking your clothes off and dancing naked on the table.

Dad and me would sometimes go out together, though he mostly went on his own. This place called 'out' seemed to weaken the hope that anybody could adapt or recover – you can talk to people but you can't make them talk back. And it was weird being alone with him. There was a distance between us, clogged up with feelings.

It was easier if Timmy or Robbie were around. Brothers come in handy, sometimes. Dad always seemed restless though.

He'd be sat at the table. He was *always* sat at the table.

This time he was going through a puzzle book. The light showed up the lines on his face. He leant with his head against his hand, shielding his eyes but screwing them up all the same. He wasn't doing much, rolling the pencil between his fingers, stopping to turn his sleeves up, pushing them to his elbows. The skin on his arms looked rough and patchy. Then he smoothed his hair back – over the thin spot, like he always does and put the pencil point against the paper as if to carry on.

'Don't stand over me,' he said, and then, kind of embarrassed he closed it, bang.

'Looks pretty difficult,' I said, because I couldn't say –

what the hell you messing with that stuff for, you're not a kid are you? He hesitated for a second, then re-opened the pages and pointed.

'Some of these take a bit of sorting out – but the crosswords – I do them against the clock, nine minutes is the record. Not too bad, seeing as I haven't bothered with any of this for years.'

I nodded. 'You could always . . . '

'I'm good at puzzles,' he said, 'specially crosswords. Used to be anyway. We should have all the old ones somewhere. I can't find any of them, p'raps you could look, you'd know where to start.'

I told him I'd look, and he smiled.

He talked about summers in the past. Looked blank as if he wasn't here, he was *there*. Went on about things I'd done and said, like I wouldn't eat eggs because they came from a chicken's ass.

I didn't listen to it though. I listened to my head.

'Women? They only want you for your bloody money,' he'd said.

'Oh yeah,' Mum'd shouted after him, 'and what is it men want – besides the slice between your waist and your knees?'

He bent down. Went about putting the fringes on the end of the rug straight 'til they looked like the teeth of a comb.

'Sometimes,' he said, 'something'll happen – I'll hear a joke, or a story or something, and I'll think to myself – I must tell her that when I get home.'

His mouth went squarish like a box. He turned away so's I couldn't see his face.

'Sorry . . . ' he said, 'I didn't mean to . . . '

I escaped to the kitchen. As I opened the door, Timmy sent his army truck speeding across the floor. It

3

stopped when it hit my foot.

'You made it crash,' he said.

I rolled it back.

'You've got chocolate all round your mouth.'

'So?' he said. 'You've got hairy armpits.'

I watched him play. Send his soldiers into battle. He'd
flick one on the head, knock it over.

'That's it. You're killed,' he'd say.

It wasn't long before Dad appeared. He stood quiet
for a few seconds. Then said to me, 'What you thinking?'

I said I was thinking about the boys working outside
– wondering if they'd nearly finished for the morning
and if I should make them some tea. Said they'd started
early and must be ready for a break. I asked him how
long he thought it'd be before a machine took over their
jobs. He said, as soon as the farm could afford it and I
told him, if I was them then, I'd save up and buy that
machine – rent it to him. He seemed satisfied, but
laughed.

I was thinking plenty of other things too.

Thinking how I didn't recognise his stories re-told.
Thinking of when I was younger and had caught him
and Mum pressed in some kind of urgent kiss sandwich.
Then thinking of her sounding tired and defeated, in a
mood that didn't match their kissing.

'If you want out, get out,' she'd said quietly.

To listen to him now you'd imagine their life together
had been perfect.

I thought about when she'd been real ill and had said
to me, 'At least you'll have him, and he'll have you.'

Then, even hearing her say that, I didn't believe she
could be ill enough to die.

4

I couldn't cut her out. Stick a label on her, 'finished'. It occurred to me that when I did something – reached eighteen, got a job, had a baby – she'd not be there to share in it. Before, I'd imagined she'd *always* be there.

Maybe this whole thing was a big lie, any minute now she'd walk in with a huge bag of cakes like she used to, hand them around. Then I remembered how once she'd slapped my face for being greedy. When I remembered bad times it seemed like it wasn't *her* I was missing now, but someone I'd never met.

It wasn't a lie. She'd left us all right, left her deadness frozen all around, the entire world exhausted by her 'going'. I was envious of anyone who still had a mother.

Sometimes I'd get a pain in the same place she'd had her pain and that made me sorry for any resentment I felt about her deserting us. Sometimes I couldn't remember what she looked like, and I'd go hot with panic.

'Where's this tea then?' Dad said.

I told him it was coming, asked him what time he was going back to work.

'The lads can cope,' he said. 'They'll be all right for the rest of the day.'

Mum would have asked him if he felt under the weather or something, so I did it. He never answered me. I went on and made the tea. The worktop was stained where I'd left the last lot of used teabags. I couldn't remember who had sugar and who didn't so I made 'general' cups – everyone had one spoonful. They'd probably complain, but so what? I was fed up with *them* and what *they* wanted.

I took some meat out of the freezer to thaw. It'd be

too much – prepared by Mum – enough for the four of us. Wished Marlene'd hurry up, she'd promised me – one o'clock, two at the *latest*. She's all right is Marlene.

I'd told her, 'I don't want to talk about it. There's nothing to say. Just treat me like normal.'

And she did. Rushed in, one minute to two.

'Okay? *Guess what happened last night?*'

'What?'

'*Guess.*'

'You were walking down the road and found ten thousand quid in a Tesco's bag?'

'No, stupid, I mean at our Mandy's engagement party.'

'Who's *Mandy*?'

'You know, me cousin – it don't matter who she is . . .'

'Where was it then?'

'In a proper night club, well, a room off it . . .'

'What was it like?'

'Stop interrupting and I'll tell you. Brill. Absolutely brill. I wore this new jersey skirt and top, looked about *eighteen*. There was this kid right, who fancied me. *You should have seen him*. Your eyes would have popped out your head. Blond hair, cropped real short, leather flying jacket, *the business*.'

'What happened?'

'I'm trying to tell you. Right. He was standing at the bar, *all* the girls giving him the once over, then he only winks at *me*, comes over and asks for a dance!'

'And?'

'And I did, course.'

'And?'

'And, *I virtually got off with him there and then*.'

'Well did you or didn't you?'

'What?'

'*Get off with him.*'

'Me Mum and Dad was there don't forget . . . '

'Boring.'

'You can say that again. But we had a few dances and all that and spent ages chatting . . . Honest, you wouldn't believe it, *he's so lush*.'

'What's he all about then? I want his whole life story.'

'Well, he's blond and . . . '

'You told me that. What's he do?'

'Nothing at the moment. Just got out of a remand centre – for fighting and that.'

'*Great.* Bet you didn't tell your Dad that.'

'Course not. Anyway he's changed now, all that's behind him. He's nothing like the wimps at school. He's really *mature*.'

'Bet he's got acne.'

'Get lost, he hasn't.'

'What else happened then?'

'*That'd be telling.*'

'Come on. Tell me.'

'Well me Mum and Dad went on to the car in a hurry 'cause me Dad felt sick. I went and got fish and chips with some others. At least that's what I told *them*.'

'Let's have the juicy details then.'

'*Mind your own,*' she said, raised her eyebrows and smirked.

'Marlene! *You didn't!*'

'Tell you what, you should have seen me Dad. Had his hand up me Mum's dress all the way home – and she was driving!'

'Don't change the subject. *Did you or didn't you?*'

'Well, I *wanted* to, definitely, but me Mum and Dad was waiting for me and that.'

'No, then?'

'But I *would've* done, I swear it. You should have heard him – he said some dead dirty stuff . . . And he was, well, *different*.'

She gazed into space. Then jumped up, rummaged through her bag, 'Look.'

'A beer mat,' I said.

'Yeah, but *look*.'

There was a name and phone number.

'His name's Mitch then?'

'Sexy innit? Said I reminded him of Kylie Minogue. And there was this other kid that fancied me too, right, Mitch was gunna smack his head in . . . '

'Never been so popular have you?'

'I could fix you up with his mate if you want.'

'No way.'

'Don't blame you. He's a prat.'

'So when you gunna ring him then?'

'Soon as me Mum and Dad are out. He wouldn't give me his number to start, right, so I got it off someone else. Tell you what, why don't you come over later on, we can phone him up – then if me Mum or Dad asks any questions I can say it's somebody to do with you, not me.'

'I can't, not really.'

'Go on. It'll be a laugh. You haven't been over for ages.'

'Can't get back.'

'Stay the night if you want.'

'But what about Timmy?'

'Your Dad can see to him.'

'Try telling *him* that.'

'Oh, go on, at least ask him.'

'I don't feel like it much anyway.'

8

'Charming.'

'Didn't mean it like that . . . '

'I know. But you will come over sometime – soon?'

'Yeah. Sometime . . . '

It wasn't just Timmy stopping me. Had some sorting out to do. I'd been putting it off, but had made up my mind to *do it* now.

Packed Mum's *best* clothes into bags. We'd promised them to a charity shop. I didn't send the normal stuff because she'd be ashamed. Checked every pocket for coins or papers, found a lot of fluff and a chocolate toffee. Some of the clothes I hadn't seen before, they were brand new, ready for her to wear when she got better.

Gave me a tight feeling in my stomach, Mum's room. Peaceful, yet it suffocated me. I held her jumper close, against my face. Held it until I wanted to rip it to pieces – *why her*?

I stuffed it into the box, crushed it down, kicked the lid closed. And all these memories kept running through my head.

Like suddenly I'm six or seven.

'Look Mum, I made you a picture!'

'I'll look later,' she says, 'I'm busy now.'

'But look! Look at my picture!'

'You mean look at the mess on that damn table.'

I study the blobs of paint on the paper. It's not very good, not really. I screw it up and throw it away. I'm no good at pictures.

Dad was always *the* one, not her. I was scared of him when I was small. If he shouted, my whole body would shudder. He'd say, 'She doesn't love her Daddy.'

I'd tell him I did, but then he'd tease and tease, so I started saying I didn't. Mum said he was 'very hurt'.

I'd asked Mum once, if they loved each other.

'Of course. Now shut up and stop being silly,' she said.

And I used to say to her, 'Do you like *me* better than . . .'

When I got to Dad and Robbie I really did want her to say 'yes', but she wouldn't. She said she liked her kids the same amount, but a husband was 'a different game altogether'. Then she'd be stroppy for ages.

At that age I used to hate being apart from her. If they were going out I'd make myself sick to try and stop her from going.

They'd go to dinner and dances quite a bit. He'd cash a big cheque and say,

'It's only money.'

Some evenings they were 'obliged' to go, even if they didn't want to. It'd worry Mum. She hated to walk into a room full of people. She'd be over-polite, put herself down, then blush. She said she didn't care what anyone else thought of her, but she did care, a lot.

She'd wear a long dress. Be cross if it was mucky outside in case the bottom got dirty before they arrived. One of her dresses, her red one, had sequins on the shoulders, she called it her 'glam' dress, but then she'd say,

'It's not over the top is it?'

Never wore any earrings or a necklace – said it was because she had glasses and would end up looking like a Christmas tree if she wasn't careful.

She had sparkly eyes.

And perfume. Always a nice one and not *too* much, though I liked her best without it. I liked *her* smell, clean and warm. Nobody else had it.

Spent ages back-combing her hair.

'Flat as a pancake,' she'd say.

Then when it was done she'd pat it down again.

'I look like an ageing Barbie doll.'

Out'd come the hair lacquer – it clung in your throat. Dad used it sometimes, but got ratty if you noticed. He doesn't like his hair, it's wiry and bushy. Robbie's is the same. Mum's was like mine, dark and smooth.

If it was a posh occasion he'd have his dinner suit cleaned, but normally he just wore an ordinary one. A blue pinstripe that made him feel like an accountant. He didn't look like an accountant, he looked stout and dated. Mum'd go up to him and undo the bottom button on his waistcoat – that's what you're meant to do, she'd say. He'd brush her aside, say he *knew that* and was just about to do it before she'd interrupted.

Always rubbed his hands together as if it was cold.

'Come on,' he'd say, 'or we'll be late – *again.*'

His head would be pointing up towards the ceiling, he'd strut around like a cockerel.

In her high heels she was taller than him. He didn't mind, unless they were having a photo taken and then he'd make her take them off, or sit down. Looked silly he said, her towering above him.

She'd wipe bits off his jacket with a damp cloth and, after one last look in the mirror, be ready to leave. Then she'd turn to us and say,

'Now don't you . . . '

'Make sure you . . . '

'If you need me, I mean if anything happens . . . '

Sometimes we were allowed to stay on our own if Mum couldn't find anyone to sit with us. She didn't like doing it, but Dad insisted that he knew *his* kids and we were 'sensible enough'. She'd phone during the evening, always ask to speak to Robbie because he was oldest and in charge.

On those nights we'd be star singers on *Top of the Pops,* with a piece of string for a microphone, and hosts on a TV game show that had gone seriously wrong, the contestants losing before eventually being crushed by the collapsing set. The world's top scientists – explaining to the ignorant masses that it *was* possible for a human being to fly like a bird and walk upside down on the ceiling like a fly. We'd be experts on every subject that existed, and we visited the moon on numerous occasions. We'd be actors in telly adverts . . . for washing powder that made things dirtier, margarine that went green as you spread it on bread . . . DIY that fell apart and cameras that exploded. We'd laughed forever.

Robbie'd tell me horror stories, hide behind the furniture and jump out on me. Tickle me until I almost wet myself. If someone knocked at the door, he'd convince me it was the mad axe man. If I went to use anything electrical he'd say,

'Touch that and . . . kaput . . . '

I believed him.

We both claimed to have seen ghosts upstairs. We both believed the other and didn't dare go up there alone.

I formed a special club. It was so exclusive, I assured him, that there was only one member. Me. But he could join if he proved himself by pulling his pants down and letting me have a look. I gasped at the turkey giblets before my eyes and dissolved the club.

They never stayed out very late. Dad wanted to but Mum wouldn't, 'in case there'd been some problem' at home.

When they got back she'd tell me all about it as I got ready for bed. Sit where she always sat – on the bean bag. Looked funny, she wasn't a bean bag type of person. Say things like the roast beef had been tough, but the baked potatoes were nice; the cabbage had been watery but the apple pie was the best she'd had in ages. She'd say if the room was smart or if it needed redecorating. What the draw prizes were and who'd won them. What the other women had on, what they'd talked about. She'd ask what we'd been up to and I'd say 'nothing'. I'd think up loads of questions so she'd stay a bit longer.

'This room's a right state again,' she'd say. 'I long for the day when these posters come down for good.'

She didn't mind them really. And she'd helped me pick out some photos to stick up. Kept one for herself. One of me sprawling on the floor, hair and clothes all scruffy. I'd wanted her to have one of the more organised ones, where I'd posed.

'No,' she said, 'this one's *you*.'

Sometimes I'd hear Dad ask if she'd enjoyed the evening. She always said, 'Wasn't bad I s'pose.'

He'd say he thought it was *really* good.

'Well,' she'd say, 'all right if you like that sort of thing.'

'No pleasing some people,' he'd mutter.

And I'd be glad to have her safely home.

It can never be like that again. I wonder what it *is* going to be like . . .

She must have been so afraid when she was being eaten up. By this thing only other people get.

And I hadn't noticed, not really, not seen it, nor felt

13

it. Maybe I just hadn't cared enough.

Our old playroom was Mum's bedroom when she got ill. Said she could rest better on her own, undisturbed. I'd plump up her pillows to make them more comfy and straighten the bed covers so's they were neat and tidy. She wanted to be tidy in case anyone should drop in to see her. I'd position the curtains so the sun wasn't in her eyes, tell her what I'd been doing, exaggerate to make it sound funnier or more serious than it had been. I think she knew. She'd smile. It seemed to take so much of her energy, just smiling. Sometimes she'd whisper, 'I'm fed up with all this. When I'm back on my feet we'll . . . '

Then she'd say some things that we'd rarely, or never done. Not too many, she couldn't manage too many. Then she'd doze.

Went into hospital for some 'little tests', came out of hospital, went back to hospital – more 'little tests', came out, exhausted.

She said she never wanted to see another white coat.

The doctor called in sometimes. I never heard what he said but according to Dad he'd say she was 'bearing up'.

Dad made her tea that she never drank, always left it on the bedside table, cold with skin on top.

A few people left chocolate and fruit she didn't want, I'd sit on the edge of her bed munching it. Telling her what had happened in *Brookside* and *Emmerdale Farm*. I told her what the newspaper said about Princess Diana's dress, and what her horoscope predicted. Timmy'd say how good he'd been. Then Dad'd tell her about the animals and the boys – though he said there wasn't much difference between the two. He told her who he'd bumped into, what they'd had to say for themselves and any spicy news.

Then we'd run out of conversation and Dad'd say, 'Oh well . . . ' and sigh.

He'd stare out of the window. I'd pick her things up from the dressing table and examine them as if they were fascinating and important.

She'd say we didn't have to stay upstairs with her, 'Go on, . . . there must be something better to occupy your evening.'

We left her. And then she was dead.

No more special times for us. No more sharing. No more making fun, telling jokes, laughing at others and at ourselves. All swept away.

I felt drained by the shock.

'She's not gone asleep *for ever* has she?' Timmy shouted. 'She's *not*. Dad says she has but he's lying and I hate him.'

Threw himself down on the bed and cried hard.

Dad was in the bathroom across the landing. The door open, I could see him at the sink, leaning over, splashing his face with water. As he stood up straight the water ran down his neck, on to his vest.

'You okay?' I asked.

'What sort of a question's that?'

And I said to myself, inside, 'It's just you now. You're on your own.' Like, everyone else was still around but your Mother's *your* Mother.

In the days following there was so much to do, but I couldn't do anything. So much to think about, but I couldn't think. It was as if a bomb had hit our lives. Blasted away our safe little unit.

Robbie came home. Helped make arrangements. Stood around looking thoughtful, twisting his moustache, speaking quietly into the telephone.

I didn't go out, couldn't face it. Dad phoned the school and told them. I lay on my bed. Didn't eat or sleep, just lay there.

'Come to say sorry – from all our lot,' Marlene said. 'What happened?'

I shrugged.

'Talk about something else.'

I'd made her feel awkward.

'What, though?'

'Anything. I don't care.'

She waffled in the background. About her family and what they'd been doing. Then, 'By the way. I want to come to the funeral, but me Mum won't let me. She's funny like that. Thinks I'm too young, that I'll get in a state. Not for you to think I'm not bothered . . . '

'That's okay.'

'You'll be all right?'

'I'll be all right.'

'What about the others – they okay?'

'Yeah . . . '

She stood up to leave.

'Thanks for coming.'

'See you soon . . . you can always ring me.'

Wasn't long since me and Mum had decided where we'd most like to travel in the world, what we'd do, who'd be there. How we'd spend a million pounds . . .

When it was time to see her, I crept into the room as if I might wake her or something.

She didn't look like her.

I touched a cheek. Didn't feel like her either. She felt hard. I didn't want to remember her this way.

Timmy was waiting for me outside.

'What'll they do with her now?' he asked.

Imagine, being trapped, underground. Imagine being burnt to ashes. I wish they could sprinkle some potion on your body and make it gradually disintegrate. Then there'd be no need to be shut tight in a box. Imagine wanting to bang your fists against the lid but being trapped *inside yourself*, with no life to do it. Calling out with no voice, like being awake under an anaesthetic – they think you're unconscious – here comes the knife.

If I'd known it was going to happen I would have tried more, treated her different. I wouldn't have kept on, wouldn't have gone out so much, would have stayed in and helped. I hardly ever helped. She said she could manage better on her own. She didn't always tell the truth though. Sometimes, when I came in unexpectedly, she might be washing-up or sewing, or reading the paper, it'd be quiet and I'd see her eyes all full. I'd ask, 'What's up?'

'Nothing,' she'd say. 'Nothing much.'

She was lying.

Even so, I wish she was still here to lie if she wanted. That day. I hate that day. That day robbed me. Knocked me over, kicked its boots into me and robbed me.

Dad kept going on about things that hadn't happened yet but might, in the future. And about how lucky we were – to live out in the country and all that.

'You know, I've been giving it some thought,' he'd said. 'When the time comes we could live in this house separately, *almost*. There'd be no point keeping the place on otherwise. Y'see we fought for this, your Mother and me. She'd not understand if I sold up.'

He stood and paced the room. I could tell he felt uncomfortable too. Put his hands in his pockets, took them out again. Clasped them together in front of himself. Then turned to look right at me.

I can't let him look at me, usually I just go, but he carried on speaking and I couldn't make myself move, not straight away.

'Robbie'd be back here like a shot if he could,' he said, 'but he's got commitments and that.'

He looked old and small.

'And there's Timmy to think about.'

'We need groceries tomorrow . . . ' I said, to change the subject.

He looked annoyed. 'You know best what to get. You can manage can't you?'

'But there's no bus on a Saturday.'

He didn't say anything. I took in, and pushed out, a big breath.

'*There's no bus on a Saturday*.'

So. I walked into town.

'*Francie*,' Marlene yelled. 'Just seen a *wicked* film. This bloke right, goes around killing these other blokes because he thinks his wife is knocking off someone else. Then he finds out it was mistaken identity but he blames her all the same, for being tarty and making him think it in the first place. Where're you going anyway?'

'Shopping.'

'Come round to our place – I taped the film – don't mind watching it again.'

'Haven't got time. Hey, what's happened about that Mitch?'

'I keep ringing him up. Keep getting his Mum, he's always out.'

'Oh well.'

'Listen, I gotta go. Our Andrew's got the plague and I'll miss the chemist. Phone you later.'

Went to just one shop – didn't traipse around for the 'best buy' like Mum would have done. Straight down the list, adding it up in my head as I went along to make sure I wouldn't be short of money when I got to the cash desk.

I got a lift back with Connie, our neighbour. She was coming up the road in her Land Rover. Called out, 'You can't carry that lot on your own – wait there – I'll go and turn around.'

Pulled up alongside me. 'How're things then?'

'Oh, okay I s'pose,' I said.

A van swerved around her, blew his horn.

'Miserable git,' she shouted, then jumped down and helped load my bags into the front. They fell over and all the shopping spilled out.

'I dunno,' she said, 'nothin's easy is it?'

'Glad I bumped into you.'

'Could have brought you in, if I'd known you were coming. Give me a ring next time t'see what I'm doing.'

We climbed in. The seats were torn and covered with bits of straw.

'This stinkin' thing wouldn't start earlier,' she said. 'Anyway, you ready?'

'I'm ready.'

'Right, away we go then . . . '

When Connie pulls off, you know about it. The ride's always a rough one. I held on to the door as she started complaining about her husband, her kids, herself.

'When I saw my reflection in the mirror this morning,' she said, 'I was *depressed*. The eyes of a drinker and a neck like a lizard.'

She was only laughing. I was going to say she hadn't got either but knowing she had both, I stayed quiet.

'Not that it matters now,' she said, 'I never was what

they'd call a cracker. I used to dream though.'

'But not any more?'

'Well, I got a good enough deal,' she said, 'or so they reckoned. Wormed my way into a decent family.'

'What's an indecent one?'

'Obvious – one with less money than your own,' and then, as if to justify herself, 'No, we've got things in common, him and me. We're a pair, a set. Got us a good life compared to some. He still buys me things you know, little presents and that,' she started laughing again and shook her head. 'Guess what he bought for me birthday last Friday – a bloody iron – I ask you. But we all get it wrong sometimes don't we?'

Her journey stopped half a mile short of mine but she said she'd drive me right the way home. I thanked her.

'Don't forget the bag down at the side love,' she said, 'I'll be seeing you.'

I struggled out, waved her off.

Connie's forty-one as well. Not very old really is it?

Timmy was waiting for me.

'Where've you been?' he said.

I pushed his fringe out of his eyes. 'I promise you can come next time.'

He scuffed up the path hanging on to my legs. 'I wet the bed last night,' he said, proud.

He helped me pack the food into the cupboard. Singing, piling the tins as high as he could until they fell over. He laughed, then looked up and said, 'Where *is* heaven? Is it in America?'

I told him it wasn't, and he said, 'Are you going there too?'

I said I thought I heard Dad calling him.

I'd visualise heaven. It didn't look that good. Posh people shaking tambourines and smiling, holding out collection boxes. Dressed up smart. Mum only had her nightie on.

I wonder if there're any flowers where she is? People sent loads of flowers when it was too late and she couldn't see them. They were left sitting there until they died too. I wished they hadn't had those tags on them, 'love from . . . ' Whose benefit is that for? Perhaps they'd like a refund in recognition.

I hated the funeral. Having to look like I was expected to – putting on a brave face, when all I wanted to do was fall apart.

Makes me shiver to think where she might be now.

I wonder if it's like being lost in a desert? If the trees are old and brittle, with rotten fruit and parasites? I wonder if there's any road back, or if it's only for certain people to use? Or what you have to do to qualify – if it still matters whether you're rich or pretty or religious? Maybe you're graded, maybe you have to accumulate points in order to move into a superior position. I s'pose you start at the bottom unless you take some points with you when you pass from alive to dead.

It's like she was swallowed by some massive hole, a crater, just a blur and that was it. Gone.

Robbie took me aside, said things'd work out, said we had to be strong. I hope Timmy doesn't grow up like him – big, serious, never in the wrong, talking *at* you.

He doesn't come home very often, he's too busy. He knows a lot more about farming than I do and I wish he didn't. Him and Dad talk about prices at market, net profit, quotas and regulations.

Dad enjoyed having someone to talk with – Robbie, or another farmer, or a local. If I was working and he was with someone, looking on and chatting, I'd go as fast as I could so's he'd be proud of me. But he never noticed. I got mad at myself for doing that. Knew I could easily be taken for granted. Like Mum. Never happened to me before, mustn't let it happen now. But I felt guilty saying 'no'. Like saying that not having Mum around to do the little grotty jobs was an inconvenience, like when a piece of equipment breaks down. He'd notice *that* and be ashamed.

Sometimes he really gets to me. Little things. Like the way he says, 'Mind you don't choke on those bones,' *every* time I eat fish.

He *always* peels apples, peaches and cucumbers . . . won't have it otherwise. He says 'slacks' instead of trousers, 'daps' instead of pumps and *cu*lculator instead of calculator.

I can't stand his hair cream or how he acts when he's nervous – not knowing where to look or what to say, clearing his throat, scuffing his feet.

Says he wants the best for me. But he says I won't have the education for a *career*, only a *job*.

Once he said, 'You'll always come to me if anything is wrong won't you?' He's the last person I'd go to if I was in trouble. I'd want to protect *him* because he'd worry much more than me.

The way he behaved at first after she'd died, I thought he had some huge secret stored up that he wanted to let me in on, but didn't know how to. Jumpy, he was, and I thought he might be going to tell me that I was adopted or something, say,

'Out of all those children, we chose *you*.'

And *I* might say,

'Big deal,' and act cool.

But *my* mother wouldn't be dead.

'Cept she is.

22

What he did finally say was that I mustn't get a chip on my shoulder. Take things as they come. That's all.

Thing is I've got to stand up for myself now because Mum can't do it for me. Mustn't let anyone push me around.

Some people might interpret *that* as having a chip on my shoulder. But whatever they say about me, I'm not taking any shit.

Two

By the time Harvest Home came around the sorrys and blushes were almost gone.

Harvest Home is *the big one* – well, if you live here it is. It's like a huge party, with a procession of floats, kids dressed in costume and a princess leading the way to a fairground. Lots of coconuts, goldfish in plastic bags and stuffed toys with staring plastic eyes.

A marquee has pride of place, the men go there for lunch, (the women are waitresses or stay outside). In the afternoon people get drunk, and in the evening there's a disco with fighting.

Everyone goes. I don't like it. It's not real – all these

people pretending to be old friends, then the minute somebody's out of sight they start slagging them off behind their back.

And I didn't want to go with Dad.

Marlene was going to be late – due back off holiday that afternoon – but he wouldn't go without me. Said he *had* to go, so I *had* to go.

'Anyway,' he said, 'someone's got to see to Timmy.'

The street was lined with faces, they'd come from all round. Dad kept telling me to push to the front so's we'd get a good view. Now and then somebody'd call out to him, nod and put their hand up.

I'd not liked to be seen out with Mum or Dad. They'd make me feel babyish if we met other kids my age who weren't with their parents. I stood a few steps away from him and pretended to be on my own. Didn't work though.

'Francie,' he said, 'for God's sake wipe your brother's nose.'

He was annoyed with me.

'Those legging things – whatever you call them – are *too tight*. And the stripy socks – they look *ridiculous*.'

There were the usual procession entries – 'Days Gone By', 'St Trinian's', 'Cops and Robbers'. Some were squirting water pistols into the crowd, the little kids loved it. Timmy joined in, 'I'm a robber, too. *I am*, aren't I Dad?'

People were agreeing with each other,

'That's the best one so far . . . '

'High standard this year . . . '

'Lots of time and effort gone into it . . . '

As the last one passed we walked to the field, to the Fair. It was muddy. There was pop music blaring from the dodgems, laughing, crying, chatter, the smell of burger and chips.

Dad paid for me to play a darts game – hit any three cards to win a cuddly toy. Then the same with shooting. I won an ornament of an Edwardian lady carrying a parasol.

Timmy starting crying,

'I want it.'

'What's the magic word?' I asked him.

He looked confused.

'Abracadabra?'

'No,' I said, 'it's *please*.'

'Well *please* then,' he said, and I gave it to him to shut him up. I tried to enjoy myself, or give that impression.

I can't stand it when you have to put on an act.

I recognised a few from school, but nobody to go round with. Helen was there, but she's more a friend of Marlene's than mine. Hadn't seen her for a while. She spoke, but we don't seem to get on like we used to.

'Waiting for Marlene?' she asked.

'Yeah. What d'you think of it?'

She shrugged.

''Salright. I'm waiting for Sal, have a muck around when she gets here.'

'Come and find me later on,' I said.

'Okay. I better go and look for her, should be here by now.'

I didn't see her after that. Maybe she didn't like the idea of Timmy tagging along.

The stall-holders were shouting non-stop –

'Try your luck . . . '

'Every one a winner . . . '

'Yes Sir – how about you . . . ?'

Women struggled with pushchairs, the wheels clogged up with grass. They moaned about prices but bought ice cream and candy floss for their children. The men soon went into the marquee to be fed. Timmy went, being a little man.

Connie wouldn't waitress like all the other women.

She told them to get knotted. She wouldn't hang about outside either and asked me back to her place for some food.

The door was on the latch, as usual – never locks it. Her dogs bounded up to meet us, jumped about, their paws all messy.

'Clear off!' she shouted.

They didn't. They wagged their tails and ran around in circles. She ignored them, pulled a tissue from her pocket and wiped their dribble off her trousers, tutting, then handing it to me to do the same.

'Look at that mark now,' she said, pointing at her leg, 'bloody dogs need shooting.'

She always wears the same type of jeans. Never seen her in a skirt. Wouldn't suit her – not with all her clumsy racing about.

The kitchen smelt of chips. She poured herself a vodka and me a coke.

'I'm giving this stuff up,' she said, 'soon – before it gives me up.'

She drank it straight down and fixed another. Rubbed her forehead. Closed her eyes for a few seconds.

'Summer hols soon be over,' she said.

'Worse luck,' I said.

I said that because it was the easiest thing to say, but I was fed up with the holidays really. Fed up with – get up, behave as if everything's normal, cook, clean, work, go to bed. Marlene had got herself a part-time job. I just fell into Mum's pattern. It dragged me down.

And school's okay anyway.

'Never mind,' Connie went on, 'only another year to go.'

'Yeah.'

'What are you – well, going to *do*?'

I told her, 'The same as other people do I s'pose. I mean, I don't know.'

'Most people aren't *doing* anything. See them lot who were there today, like they just go along with it all, they just *exist*, they don't *do*. I don't *do* . . . not really.'

'You can't always have it the way you want though can you?' I said. 'Why not?' she said. 'Why does it matter what other people say or think? I reckon you *can* have it your way.'

I told her about *them*, those who get paid to 'guide' you, put you in your pigeon-hole. Careers Advisers they call themselves.

I'd said, 'I definitely want to do art,' and they glared down at me, behind their *big* desk, leaning back in their *big* chairs.

'How about hairdressing or clerical?'

'Art.'

'But that's not realistic is it? And it's not all it's made out to be, the competition's tough. You'd only waste three years or more. So shall we put you down for hairdressing or clerical?'

'It used to be easy,' Connie said, 'because there was no choice.'

She didn't look sad, or angry, or anything. Twisted a strand of her bottle-blond hair. Let it go. Did it again.

'I got married. That's what everyone did. Without thinking, we just did it. Then we were too proud to let anyone know if we needed help. Like a Punch and Judy show it was.' She paused. 'Let's not sit here, let's eat

28

then walk . . . , or *something*.'

She took two pasties from the fridge and unwrapped them, said for me to get the plates. Mum had always teased Connie about her kitchen, it's like a bomb site. Nothing's got a particular place, things live where they were last used. She was searching for clean knives and forks, couldn't find any so washed some up.

'Remember last year when we did this?' I asked.

'Yeah,' she said, 'hard not to.'

She wiped the cutlery and handed it to me. I took a mouthful of pastie and swallowed. Then, without looking at her, I said, 'Did you ever see that thing in the paper? About Mum?'

'Yeah, I did.'

'I cut it out. I look at it sometimes.'

She stopped eating and looked at me.

'Just "was born and lived in the village all her life – has died",' I said, 'as though that's all there was to it.'

She nodded.

'What d'they know?' she said. Then 'Not much,' and looked sad.

'And at the funeral,' I said, 'the vicar talking. He didn't *know* about her. Nor did most of the people there. I didn't want them there . . . '

Silence for a minute or so.

'I miss her too,' she said, 'really do.'

We walked down the lane, away from the noise. Walked without speaking. It was hot. Connie huffed and puffed over a cigarette. Beads of sweat glistened on her face, through her thick foundation cream that Mum used to call Polyfilla.

When we reached the gate leading to the Perrys' farm, she stopped. Climbed on to the bottom bar.

I had the wrong clothes on, felt sticky. Connie

untucked her shirt, tied it at the waist, showing an inch or so of belly. It poked out like a thin tyre. Her jeans looked tight around the middle, I bet they left a red mark when she took them off. I hitched my top up, but I hate the way my stomach's all rounded so I put it back to how it was before. Decided to suffer.

Stood looking but not looking really.

'There must have been *something* they could have done,' I said, 'those doctors. There *must* have been.'

'Don't think so,' she said.

Then, 'I wish there was something *I* could do – to make it better for you.'

I felt tingly.

Later on, back home, Dad said, 'What did *she* want with *you* all afternoon?'

'Nothing.'

'What did you do then? What did you talk about? Two people can't do *nothing* for four hours.'

I said, 'Nothing.'

And he said, 'I don't want you mixing with people like *that* – she's . . . '

He didn't say what.

'*You* mix with her,' I said, fed up.

'That's different.'

He looked upset. I wondered if he kept his 'deeply wounded' face in a box under the bed, took it out when he felt the moment required it.

'I know,' he said, 'let's get a video for tonight. A good one. We can go out first if you want, watch it when we get home. What d'you want to do? Say . . . '

We drove back to the marquee. Timmy was being a pain. Picked the scab on his knee until it bled, then whined because I didn't have a plaster. It'd gone off chilly and was spitting with rain. The field was cluttered with chip papers, empty cans and litter.

'By the way, your mate 'phoned. Marlene.'

'When? Is she coming down then?'

'Didn't ask her.'

'Why didn't you tell me before?'

'Well I wouldn't have thought she'd be out tonight, only just got back home.'

'That's not the point.'

'Oh, don't start. Don't have to live in each others' pocket do you . . . '

It was busy, the girls' high heels were sinking in the mud and a fusty pong came from the men's suits, mothballs. One girl, Bev, came rushing over to us. She smiled as she kissed Dad on the cheek, and said, 'See you for a dance later.'

I was jealous.

'I don't want to stay long. We could pick up a film in town if we hurry.'

'Plenty of time,' he said.

I told him I didn't feel well, maybe I'd go home on my own.

'You won't,' he said, 'not with these idiots about. We'll put in an appearance, then go. 'We're bound to show some support, just for a few minutes.'

The music wasn't bad. Except for the occasional 'funny' song slipped in. The tent was decorated with flowers, some boys were pulling them down, holding them between their teeth and prancing around in a 'look at me' way. In the corner a boy and girl were kissing, another pair were having a row. They made it up when a slow record came on.

There was lots of –

'Haven't seen you for ages.'

'Come and have a drink with us.'

'What're you up to now?'

Dad chatted to a few people about nothing much. Timmy crawled about on his hands and knees pretending to be drunk. I told him not to be so stupid.

'You smell,' he said.

'Leave him alone,' Dad said. 'He's not doing any harm.'

'Yeah, *leave me alone*,' he said, real smug.

Marlene was fuming.

'*Half-past six* we got back. They *knew* I wanted to be back *early*. *Then* they say I've got to be in by *ten*. Ten!'

'How was sunny Yorkshire?'

'Don't ask. And I bet Mitch tried to 'phone me while I was away . . .'

'It's been rubbish here . . .'

'Yeah? *I hate it around here.* Y'know, I've made up my mind – as soon as I'm sixteen I'm going on the pill – as soon as I'm seventeen I'm learning to drive – and as soon as I'm eighteen I'm going grape picking in the South of France.'

'Sea, sand and sun . . .'

'And sex. Our Mother's right, she's such a cow. She promised I could have a new swimming cossie as soon as we got to Yorkshire. *You should have seen the one she made me have.* I wanted one cut high on the legs with a zip-up front. She said "zip-*up* front, zip-*down* front. You're not having it". Ended up with this pretty pink thing that looks like a five year old's.'

'Come on Francie,' Dad said, 'we're going.'

'What, already?'

'It was *you* that *wanted* to go . . .'

'Well I don't now.'

'*Come on*, I've had enough of your messing about.'

'No.'

He caught hold of my arm, 'I won't tell you again young lady.'

'Well I don't care anyway. It's crap here.'

I said goodbye to Marlene, followed him outside. It was still light.

He ran his fingers over a scratch on the car.

'*How long's that been there?*' he said, shaking his head. 'Somebody's been and done that while we were in the tent. Bloody yobs.'

He slammed the door hard. Calmed down a bit, then said, 'Apparently, Sheila's daughter is *expecting*.'

'Expecting what? A miracle?' I said.

'Very clever. She's ruined now. Absolutely ruined.'

'Who *did the dirty deed* then?'

'If you mean who's the father, I don't know. Still, if that's the kind of girl she is, I doubt she knows either.'

'Might not even be true.'

'Well Joss told me – he's no reason to say it if it wasn't right. Like he said, she's not much older than you. Silly girl, *silly girl*.'

'She might *want* a baby.'

'Course she doesn't.'

'Then why doesn't she have an abortion?'

'I'll forget you ever said *that*.'

Then, 'Joss asked me – what's your Francie going to do then?'

Who knows?' I said.

'Wait and see. I might do a lot, then again, I mightn't.'

'Kate's daughter went gallivanting off,' he sneered, ' . . . thought she knew it all. But she soon came back, head hanging down.'

'*I'm* gunna be a farmer,' Timmy said.

We picked up a video but I didn't feel like watching it.

Didn't feel like doing anything lately.

I wished there was someone to blame, say,

'Things would never have turned out this way if *you* hadn't made it happen.'

But there wasn't anybody.

'I don't know what to do with you sometimes,' he said.

'Sorry I didn't come with instructions.'

He shrugged, then smiled.

'No. But you used to think you had *Made in Hong Kong* stamped on your back – when you were four or five, 'member?'

'So what?'

'So, they were good days weren't they?'

I wonder where I *was* made? Probably on the bedroom floor after the annual Farmers Union cabaret night. I overheard him saying once, 'There *is* such a thing as lust y'know.'

She'd replied. 'Yeah? Your brain's between your legs.'

I slumped in the chair, sulky and miserable. Picked the loose piping around the cushion, then thought better of it. Dad went and sat with Timmy. Lit a cigar and coughed a bit.

The room soon filled with smoke. Mum didn't like him smoking in the lounge, said it made the curtains and all that real smelly. Dad said it wasn't his smoking that done it, it was having a log fire. I think he was just getting at her – she'd kept on and on until he'd opened the fireplace up, built around it in stone. Well, he didn't actually *do it* – he gave the go-ahead. Reluctantly. They had the whole room done out in blues and cream. The sofa and chairs had been re-covered in a flowery material – but not tacky-flowery. Looked good.

He started the film off then leant back, plonking his feet on the coffee table.

'Sylvester Stallone,' he said to me. 'You'd enjoy this.'

I left them to it. Went and sat in the dining room.

I'd go in there because no one else ever did. I could get away in there.

It smelt damp. Hadn't been touched for years, never got used, more of a junk room. Boxes, odd bits of furniture, accounts books and papers piled on the floor.

Didn't put the light on, didn't want it on. Sat on the window ledge, looked out into the yard. The boys hadn't picked up the empty feed sacks, they'd be in trouble for that.

You could hear the disco easily and see a glow from the lights all around.

'Go for it Sly!' Dad was shouting. 'Go for it boy!'

'I'm gunna be a boxer, Dad,' Timmy was saying.

An echoey voice came over the PA system from the marquee,

'Bouncers to the front of the stage please.'

('Bloody troublemakers,' Dad'd say tomorrow, 'louts, spoil it for everybody.')

'*Please – more bouncers and medical assistance at the front of the stage.*'

('When the drink's in, the sense is out,' he'd say tomorrow.)

'*Police – please – to the front of the stage.*'

('Short sharp shock, that's what the buggers need,' he'd say tomorrow.)

'Yeah!' Dad shouted. Sly was thumping his opponent in time to the music.

('What a movie!' he'd say tomorrow. 'What a man!')

Outside I could just make out two figures emerging from the barn. It was Alex, one of Dad's labourers and

Linda, a girl from the village. They were straightening their clothes. She put her arm around him, he said something, shook her off.

('What a screw!' he'd say tomorrow.)

When Alex can't think of anything else to say to me, he usually says, 'Oh no! It's the Communist. Alert, reds approaching!' Then he mimicks a warning siren.

I give him a Nazi salute, but say very little. Matt, the other kid, tells me to ignore him. Like he says, they're all slightly right of extreme fascism around here. The locals don't approve of anything that differs.

'Show me so-called progress and I'll show you a foul-up,' they say.

Mum would never let on where her preferences lay, a closet socialist perhaps?

She wasn't like the rest in some ways. *She* never closed her mind to new ideas, just thought they were out of *her* reach, so tried to convince herself that her life was all right *really*.

Once, I heard her say to Connie, 'At least I've got my kids,' as if *we* were her achievement.

Connie often talks to me about *her* kids.

'They get on your nerves some days. Most days.' Then she thought about it. 'But not *every* day, I don't s'pose.'

'Not when they're asleep.'

'That's right. I've got no complaints then. *But I wouldn't be without them, that's for sure*. You end up living your life through your kids – if Pete or Lizzy or Jude do something good I feel, well, satisfied. You've done your bit, they've done theirs. It's the same with *him* really. If he manages to buy another piece of land, or something new, big, for the farm, I get a good feeling. It means we're doing all right.'

She always spoke of her husband as if he was one of her kids. He didn't *look* like one mind you. The big strong guy and his woman.

'I'm really getting to *know* them now,' she said, 'there never was time before. 'Cept now they're leaving, going their own ways.'

'Don't seem fair,' I said, 'not on anybody.'

'No. But there was work to be done and if you don't work you don't get money, so you don't eat and you don't wear clothes, only rags. So you work. In a way, I begrudged them being there, needing me, putting so much pressure on us like that. Don't get me wrong – I love them kids, but that's the way it was. That's why we don't seem, well, friends I s'pose. I wanted to be with them – I *did* – but food has to come first. Still,' she finished, 'them days are over.'

She reached into her bag and brought out a five-pound note.

'Here, buy something nice – it's all right, go on.' She smiled, 'I took it out of his trouser pocket this morning, he never notices.'

I scrunched it up in my hand.

'You sure?'

'Don't ever ask that,' she said, 'I could say "no I'm not sure," and whip it back. It's a gift. From me to you.'

I pushed it deep into my pocket. Connie snapped her bag shut, a square, old-fashioned thing with a noisy gold clasp.

'Glad we sorted that out,' she said, smiling.

If Mum had heard, she'd frown. Dad wouldn't like it either. He'd say it'd look like he couldn't afford to keep me properly himself. And Mum used to say, 'Never show a man up – unless it's trouble you're asking for.'

He didn't like her to have too much cash at hand. Said

37

she had the run of the cheque book, but if she used one he'd want to know on what, where, why and would demand, '*How* much?'

He gave her a 'wage', but said things like, 'He who pays the piper calls the tune.'

I know a better one.

'He who controls the purse controls the person.'

Her only aim was to keep us all fed, clean and safe – not even happy really, being happy was up to the individual. A bonus. She was scared to let me do some things in case I got hurt – like, she wouldn't let me learn to swim in case I drowned in the process. But she wanted to teach me all she knew. And what she knew was farming.

She'd explain – how things worked, how to go about repairing things rather than renewing them. She'd tell me what symptoms an animal had – what it might mean – how they'd cure it. How to prevent waste, prevent accidents.

She always wore what she called 'the sensible thing' for work. Stretchy crimplene trousers with the seams sewn in. Courtelle jumpers in pastel shades. Yuk. But I hadn't been able to throw them in the bin.

Marlene says I've got the same figure as Mum. Not too fat, not too thin.

'Not like me. I'm *fat* aren't I? Gross.'

'You're not that bad.'

'Come on, say it. I can take it – *Marlene you're gross.*'

'Go on a diet then.'

'Nah. Diets never work on me. I might do me Mum's Jane Fonda workout though.'

She looked at herself in the mirror.

'What d'you think's my best feature? Me eyes I s'pose. Or lips? I know I've got a good personality – me auntie reckons I'd be good at working with people, if I smartened me voice up. Could be a *hotel receptionist* or something. Work in a really posh place where all the stars stay. Might even get off with one of them . . . '

'What happened to the South of France?'

'*After* the South of France. I mean, I can't stay there for ever. What d'you think about this hair colour anyway – you haven't said anything. Honey blond it's called, like it?'

''Sall right.'

''Orrible innit? It's wash-out but I can't be bothered to do it. D'you know me Mum reckons I'm allergic to white flour and that's why I'm lazy . . . '

Timmy came in.

'Marlene. I don't like you.'

'Sod off then,' she said.

'I'm telling Dad of you.'

'He's not here, he's run away and is never coming back 'cos you're such a pain.'

He began to cry.

'Sorry,' she said to me, 'I didn't think. Didn't mean to make him cry. I'm *never* having kids.'

'He's only little,' I said.

When I was little I'd say to Mum, 'I love you as big as this house, as big as this country, as big as this world.'

'Now come on,' she'd say, 'eat your supper and stop fooling around.'

Dad might turn up for supper at any time between six and eleven. He might have been sorting out some emergency, but more than likely he'd been 'caught up' talking in the pub. He'd moan if there was no food put back for him. He'd moan if there was, too. Say it was dried up.

'Shouldn't those kids be in bed?' he'd ask.

'They wanted to watch something on telly.'

'They rule this house.'

'At least they're someone to talk to.'

'Here we go.'

'It's true.'

'Don't think of *them* will you?'

'They like staying up.'

'*You* like them staying up.'

'Yeah – I get lonely here – but there's no harm done is there?'

'No good done either.'

'*You* just want them out of your way.'

'And *you* should have bought a couple of puppies instead.'

'Oh, not much difference. I mean they're an inconvenience, and leak at both ends.'

He'd grip her tight by the arms, clenching his teeth together, and say, 'Thank Christ I'm a patient man.'

But then, if he did ever try to do something with us, join in, show us something, she'd barge in, '*I'll* show them.'

If she ever got us a present, he'd grin, 'But wait 'till you see the one *I've* got for you.'

'Plastic rubbish,' she'd say.

'Maybe, *but look how they love it*,' he'd answer.

They could be enemies with each other, but as far as we were concerned they were together. Quite often he'd say to us, 'You speak badly of your Mother and I'll knock you into next week.'

And her, 'That man is your Father – don't you *ever* forget that.'

Try to divide them – no chance. Like the moment you divulge some sin to one of them, and say, ' . . but

40

don't tell . . . '

Before you know it, in a voice loud enough to muffle a Boeing 747, 'What? Don't tell *who*? Why not?'

Who then jumps to his or her feet and springs on to the scene.

'Did I hear my name mentioned?'

'No,' you say. But it's too late.

'What's going on?'

'Well I'm not quite sure, you'd better ask your daughter . . . '

By this stage you're wishing you were a garden gnome with herpes, or somebody, *anybody* else.

'You what?' they say, (the bewildered expression should be recorded and used for reference at RADA).

'Where *did we* go wrong?'

They shake their heads in unison.

And all you said was . . . 'Can I borrow two-fifty?'

God doesn't mess around arguing. He just pokes his head out of the sky and says, 'I want that one. Give her something terrible and send her up (or down) at the end of the year.'

I've wondered what'd happen if Dad suddenly collapsed in a heap, dead.

Said that to Marlene.

'He won't,' she said.

'How do you know? He might.'

She hesitated.

'You don't talk about your Mum much.'

'No. Because nobody's got the answers to my questions.'

'What questions?'

'Like where the hell is she? Is she just lying in the ground rotting or what?'

41

'That's awful,' she said. 'Spooky.'

People often mistook me for Mum on the phone – customers and suppliers. I took it as a compliment and dealt with them in the way that she would have. But no matter how you go about things, there's always a chunk missing. It felt like it does when you stay in somebody else's house. It was too quiet so I kept the radio on the whole time to make a bit of noise. Pretended to be tired and went to bed early.

But the gossips and stirrers played on my mind. For a start there were the 'Vidal Sassoons meet Hilda Ogdens'. They'd seen me and lowered their voices, though I could still hear them.

'Their place not up for sale then?'

'Not as far as I know.'

'Thought it might be.'

'They'd get a fair bit.'

'How much d'you reckon he's worth?'

'Enough to make him a fair old catch.'

'I heard he's still on tablets.'

'He ought to take on a housekeeper, a nice little red-head, that'd soon make him feel better.'

'You volunteering?'

'I wouldn't be his first.'

'Nor his last.'

'Somebody reckoned – only don't say I said – that Mrs tried to do away with herself once.'

'Is that right? No wonder he's on tablets.'

'You never know do you, what goes on behind closed doors?'

I was pretending to look at style books. Furious with myself for not having the courage to speak up.

When it came to my turn their voices returned to normal level.

'How's you love?'

'All right.'

'And Dad?'

'All right.'

'We were saying about your Mum the other day – what a smart woman she could be when she dressed up and that.'

'Had some good clothes,' dogsbody chirped up. 'I remember seeing her in that navy and white suit . . . '

'It's always a job to know what to do with personal belongings, clothes . . . '

'We gave them away,' I said.

'What a waste.'

'To poorer people.'

'Even so, it's a shame . . . '

For a second I pictured the rubber roll-on girdles and big knickers that we didn't send.

'Dad busy?'

'Seems to be.'

'Best thing in the circumstances. Never was afraid of getting blisters on his hands.'

To which dogsbody added, 'No. Good with his hands' (giggle).

'I liked your Mother.'

She didn't like *them*. They intimidated her. She'd talk about them, then say,

'Still, I was at the back of the queue when looks were given out.'

But *they* were the ugly ones. With ugly hearts. In an ugly shop they had the bottle to call a *salon*.

It was shabby, grubby pink walls and upholstery. Smelt of perm lotion. There were loads of advertising photos showing glamorous plastic women – as if, 'you too could look like this with a snip of the scissors.'

She ran her fingers through my hair, her long painted nails scratching my head.

'What *have you* done to it?'

She had a nerve, hers was like a mane of fluffy cotton wool.

'I wanted it this colour,' I said.

'Jet black – like a little foreign girl?'

'What's wrong with that?' I said and she raised her eyebrows in disapproval.

'And,' I said, 'I want it long at the front and short at the back.'

'Well. I don't think so, it won't suit you, it'll look funny. I'll do what I can love.'

She did what she could. It wasn't funny. Well, it was as funny as Ronald Reagan.

My heart jumped when I looked in the mirror properly, front, back and sides. She'd done it how I'd told her to. It didn't suit my face at all, but it was drastic and suited my feelings.

'What's your Dad gunna think?'

'Who cares?'

As I was leaving I heard dogsbody whisper, 'Gunna be trouble that one.'

Dad cut my hair once. I'd been lying upside down on the settee, chewing bubble-gum when it fell out of my mouth, into my hair. I pulled it, tried to get it out, but it had the opposite effect and made it more or less permanent. Being knowledgeable on such matters, I didn't go to Mum. Dad had been watching anyway. And he'd seen it as a 'that'll teach you', rather than a mega disaster. He got the sharpest knife from the drawer, sliced the matted clump out in one go. Then he told Mum as I tried to make bargains with God.

Funny how you believe in God *sometimes*.

'*Why didn't you use scissors?*' she screamed at him. I was glad he hadn't because now it meant he was getting the rollocking, not me. 'For Christ's sake,' he said, 'I'm not a bloody stylist.'

I must admit, I can't imagine him standing around with a brush and comb in his hand, gossiping with *them* two about 'heavy flow' and what the doctor said at dogsbody's internal (nice ovaries apparently).

Mum and Dad used to 'have words' quite often.

I used to argue with Mum too. She'd irritate me sometimes, though I feel bad about that now.

She used to buy my clothes because she said I could only be trusted to come home with a bag full of tatty rubbish. *Quality* was something that I appeared to know nothing about. She bought the most hideous things ever produced, but because they were expensive it seemed they were superior to *fashion*.

I remember a jumper with *embroidered roses*, and a mac with a huge collar when everyone else's was almost non-existent, pencil thin.

And always too big, in case I grew overnight.

If I bought anything for myself and it shrank or broke, she'd say, 'Well it was obvious wasn't it . . . ?' But if she'd bought it she'd accuse me of not looking after it properly.

Loads of things she did got to me. She always went 'Huh', and laughed when something was important. She'd sit picking bobbles off socks. And insisted on sticking knitting needles in plant pots 'for support', like it could be the strongest plant in existence but she had to do it, *just in case* it decided to go floppy.

And she was impatient. She'd say things like, 'There *is* no excuse,' and 'it's all down to you my girl.' Without

45

stopping to weigh anything up she'd say, 'If the swines get you down it's because you let them.'

She can make me feel guilty even now, about things I did *years* ago – things she didn't know about. She had no time for wrong doings.

She was proud, she insisted, to have been 'as a nun' on her wedding day.

Though she used to enjoy Connie's secrets.

' . . . and he said, "We'll have to hurry or your old man'll catch us." Then about three seconds later, I asked him, "*Was that it*? No," I said, "it was all right really. Better when I had my eyes closed though!" He only laughed. Squeezed me like a slice of lemon over a prawn cocktail he did.'

I've never had a squeeze like that. I've had a kiss where your mouth stays firmly shut and your head moves about a lot. And a tonguey French kiss that bore no resemblance to midnight in Paris. A slug in a cave more like. I was pressed up against a wall at the time, outside, in the drizzle.

'I reckon I'm in with a chance aren't I?' he'd said to me.

Marlene was a few feet away with some other creep:

'I'm gunna be a model y'know.'

'Yeah?'

'Earn loads of dosh.'

'Topless?'

'No – fashion. Dead sophisticated . . . '

That was at the first Football Club disco I was allowed to go to. Not on my own – the oldies went too. I don't know how I managed to escape from them for those few minutes, they must have been into their weird dancing – you know, not moving their feet, but swinging their arms a lot. Let's face it, they've got no idea

46

have they? A couple of drinks and it turns into an *Opportunity Knocks* audition.

It was in the village hall – a rectangular box with no atmosphere and blocked toilets. Sounds hollow when footsteps cross the wooden floor. They draw the curtains, dim the lights, set up a table to act as a bar and off they go.

'Sixties,' they shout, 'play some sixties stuff.'

Bloody hippies.

'No – fifties,' somebody shouts.

Fifties – can you believe it?

'*Elvis*!'

Elvis who?

Mum loved music. She didn't sing much though.

But she was never going to die, that's for sure. It takes a while to convince yourself that the walls aren't actually going to fall in and bury you too.

I used to laugh at her behind my hands. But now, if I dared cry for her, I would never stop.

I'm seven or eight again: 'Let's play . . . '

'I'm worn out.'

'Where's Dad?'

'Out.'

'Let's play, go on . . . '

'*I'm tired.*'

Then I'm eleven or twelve: 'Why is it,' she said, 'that you'll never do as I tell you? You always have to *negotiate terms . . .* '

If she could have seen the way I looked now, she'd have throttled me.

'*Groo-vy,*' Marlene said. 'Your Dad's gunna *kill* you.'

I was standing in the yard when he'd glared in the

general direction of my head and gone wild.

'You're not to leave these premises unless I say so. How can I let you out on the street looking like *that*?'

He wasn't the only one who thought it his business.

'Wouldn't want to sleep with *you* tonight,' Alex said.

'Wouldn't want to sleep with *you* any night,' I snapped back.

'You could go blonde. You'd look like Marilyn Monroe then,' pause, 'after the autopsy.'

'Did I ever tell you,' I said, 'that your great conquest, *Linda*, swears she'd rather sit on her finger?'

Dad heard, 'You disappoint me,' he said, 'you talk like some slut.'

I wonder what he sees in his head when he's angry, or when he's upset? Or how he feels when he looks at something horrid or cruel, or something beautiful?

When he's by himself, he's lost. But as soon as he gets with other men he's a part of it all. I don't know which is the real him and which isn't.

At my age he actually *owns* me. It's as if I'm too young to have needs.

You know I wouldn't be surprised to find out that parents are a big mistake, a design fault. Like, if I ever went to them with some kind of problem, and said, 'What shall I do about this?'

Dad would say, 'That's your Mother's department.'

So I'd go to her, 'What shall I do about this?'

'Ask your father.'

'He said ask you.'

'*Is your neck clean?*'

' . . . but what about . . . '

'No, it's not. Wash it *now*.'

' . . . but what about . . . '

'Never mind that.'

48

If she ever got hold of you with the flannel – look out. Wasn't satisfied unless she'd gone round your eardrums and rubbed your skin raw (yeah, I know, you could plant potatoes in that amount of dirt).

Cleaned the house until it started wearing away. Always moved things, got behind them, under them with the hoover. I mean, what *is* the point? Who's going to come into your home, turn the sofa on its side, scratch the carpet, examine their fingers, then say, '*Dust*. This is *dust*, you filthy grub of a person.'

Who?

Her first acknowledgment of me *getting older* was a can of anti-perspirant. Then came a truly vital piece of information – I'd need to change my knickers more often. Well, fancy that.

She had *total* belief in germs. Lurking everywhere, waiting to pounce. When I was a baby I'd be merrily picking my nose when she'd knock my hand away at a hundred miles an hour, screaming that word,

'GERMS.'

If you ever got a *cold* she'd say, 'Where've you been to catch *that*?'

Our place of course was *far* too clean to harbour such terrible things.

I was never a separate person from Mum, I was always an extension of her.

If I asked for, say, different food, she'd go, 'That mucked up stuff? I don't buy it because you wouldn't like it.'

I'd say, 'But how do you know that?'

'I just do,' maybe adding, 'so shut up, and eat what you've got.' *She* didn't like it, so *I* wouldn't.

She'd say I was ungrateful. Every time I asked for lasagne – or a faded denim jacket – she'd say I was

49

ungrateful. Never did my street cred any favours.

I tried to impress her. Tell her if I'd done well in an exam or in sports.

'Well,' she'd say, 'it *must* have been easy.'

She always pissed on my fireworks.

Sometimes I wished they'd dump me in some awful place so's I had some incriminating evidence against them – to spite them for not taking notice of the things I did well. And I used to fantasise about having a different family.

You're not meant to criticise your parents. It's different when you're small. People think it's cute, then laugh and call you a cheeky little devil.

Marlene told me once that men used to hang garlic around their wobbly bits to fend off the devil. She read it in the paper. I wonder if he's been planted in our imaginations just to make us watch our step. He's s'posed to live in hell isn't he? Where it's flame hot and packed with wasters.

Probably Benidorm.

No way is Mum in hell.

I wish I didn't put her and Dad down. I don't mean to say there's not a lot of good in them, there is.

And I never told her that I, well, you know, loved her—not often enough anyway. She never told me either. P'raps she didn't. She must have. But if you say stuff like that they take the piss out of you and you're laughed at. Makes you feel like saying,

'In actual fact, I hate your friggin' guts.'

Get your own back on them. Make them angry – physical contact, a slap around the ear.

'Pressure,' she used to say, 'damn (never even *bloody*) pressure. *Just get on with it.*'

Get on with what though? Living for the sake of it,

until you die? What about in between?

The thing is, they do the telling, and it's unchallenge-able as far as they're concerned. You don't know anything.

Parents hold an invisible power. There's always a chance that they're psychic. They've sussed you *and-just-you-wait-madam*.

Like you're at the *planning* stage of what to wear somewhere, going over it in your mind, having said nil.

'What's the matter with you?'

'Nothing.'

(Hair. You're thinking about hair. What can you stick on it? Some of that red food colour, streak it . . . ?)

'There is *something*.'

'No there's not.'

(Make-up. What can you slap on your face? Bright red lipstick to go with the hair . . .)

'What've you *done*?'

'*Nothing*.'

(Clothes. Could wear the dress that's too big, let it hang off one shoulder, real cool . . .)

'Nothing *yet*,' they say.

No recipe for a social life is it? And you try *discussing* it. Strong words develop – a state of emergency de-clared. Brief exchanges of opinion – a curfew imposed. The final conflict – imprisonment without fair trial, loss of privileges. Solitary confinement *if you're lucky*. I'm only glad capital punishment was abolished.

It's almost as if they're jealous. *They're* stuck in being bored, so you should be too. Mum used to say, 'There's not a jealous thread in my body,' before she ran someone into the ground.

Dad'd got worse since she died. Wound up about where I was, who I was with, what I was *getting up to*.

51

I was only hanging around with Marlene. There's this bus shelter in the village – it sort of belongs to *us*. We sit there for hours chatting, watching people drive by.

'Look at that bitch staring at me,' she said.

'D'you know her?'

'No. But I'll give her somethin' to stare at if she's not careful.'

'What were you saying about your Dad?'

'Got arrested. Last night. For nicking. Well, he wasn't *really* nicking – he was gunna put the money back – only borrowed it. Me Mum had been saying it's not long to Christmas and going on about how much it costs, and he said he felt he ought to be bringing more in. Like she made him feel useless. She blames herself. She's gunna say that in court. He thinks she ought to – might help to get him off.'

'Is he home now then?'

'On bail.'

Dad didn't like Marlene because of her Dad. Said trouble runs in her family. She's not trouble, just a good laugh. In school she caused an explosion in the chemistry lab – we nearly wet ourselves laughing. And when we weren't allowed inside to the loos at dinner time, she said to the teacher on duty,

'But, Sir, I need to change my tampon.'

You should have seen his face – he nearly died of shock, talk about embarrassed. We creased up. We'd giggle and muck around worse than Timmy.

Her Mum calls us the twins, because we wear the same kind of clothes. Dad said the other day that I'm getting to look like my Mum.

'I didn't realise you had legs until you wore those shorts on Sunday,' he said.

He likes me to *make the most of myself*. With limits. He

doesn't like it when I wear lipstick or eyeliner, but a bow in my hair is fine, if you see what I mean.

I'm not tall like Mum. But I feel tall sometimes.

I wonder what she does all day now? Maybe creeps around, smiling but scared? Maybe looking for people she knows. Imagine that never-ending searching.

And since she got ill she couldn't even manage to walk far.

I can't imagine Mum with any other man except Dad. It would have been him, or no one. I said to Robbie, 'D'you think they were *happy*?'

'*Of course they were happy*, what makes you ask *that*?'

But I reckon they were just admiring the view. Weren't happy together, but wouldn't have been happy apart either. Whatever happy is. Being content? Being discontent but allowed to challenge? Or being free, able to be yourself?

Seems like most of the time we're just drifting. As if *now* is just a rehearsal for something better.

Three

Time dragged slow without Mum. Like we were waiting. Waiting for-I-don't-know-what to happen.

I'd go out with Marlene. P'raps I shouldn't have. P'raps I should have stayed in with Dad. He was real moody.

'I don't know how to handle you,' he said, 'I don't know what you expect, what you want. You just keep on for more.'

Sometimes he wouldn't speak to me at all.

I'm not sure if I *did* keep on that much. I don't *think* I did. I didn't mean to, and I really tried not to. I tried to be what he wanted. 'Cept I could never be that.

He expected me to be a younger version of Mum. Fit into the space she'd left behind. Clean his clothes, cook his food, tidy up after him.

'*Why isn't it done?*' he'd say.

'Because you haven't done it.'

'Don't you think *I* do *enough*?'

I'd tell him that I looked after myself, why couldn't he do the same.

'Oh, I'm all right Jack.'

I'd argue that we *both* had to do things, but his answer was always the same,

'Why d'you have to make it so hard? Why can't you make an effort?'

He wouldn't go to work.

Kept wandering around the house – checking up, double checking that everything was as it should be – things turned off properly, tap not dripping, ashtrays safe.

Once he shouted:

'You make this place look like a pigsty,' when I hadn't, and I was *going* to tell him – don't worry, you won't have to shout much longer, do anything you feel like doing, *just get me away from you* – that's what I was *going* to say, started to say, but stopped.

He was holding on to the table, hands shaking, his face all wet with crying. He was in *bits*. I didn't dare go near or break the silence.

Not my Dad. That was a man I didn't know, a stranger in my Dad's body. He ran out.

What's the scramble inside of him say? Does it hurt, hurt like you're being shredded into tiny pieces? Is it empty, is it cold?

Can I make him warm again?

I wish I could ask him. But it'd be like asking

someone to shoot us in the heart, just to see how well we survived.

We don't talk real and we don't touch. Not ever. Not *ever*.

I want to talk. I want to touch.

When I was little, I wanted to marry him.

'No,' he said, 'you're only *saying* that.'

Am I only 'saying' this? Don't I mean it?

Don't I care what happens to him?

Should I run and tell him it's okay, it'll be different from now on because I'm going to . . . what? Change the past?

I'm tugged backwards again. A long way.

'Look at the state of your clothes – you *bad* girl.'

'I told you not to do that – why don't you listen?'

'You're so bloody defiant – what's wrong with you?'

I'm sorry. I *am* sorry.

'Good girl Francie, bring Dad his cigarettes. Good girl.'

'Dad's girl, that's what you are.'

When you've got no idea what to do, what *should* you do?

Just try and be there? 'Cept how d'you let someone know you're there when you feel like you're on another planet. Cooped up with aliens and ruled by land-mines.

Mum's dying was like being forced into something obscene. *Can't* accept it. You fight and struggle. *You're* the only weapon you can use against giving up, but you never needed you 'till now. Don't know how it works.

Felt like I was playing somebody else's part, except I couldn't go home and change. Change back into how it was before.

We never mentioned what happened.

I was going to say something to Connie, but she was busy. Shovelling muck. Looked up without stopping, moving like clockwork,

'I'll see you another time – can't stop now love.'

I was hurt. Disappointed that she couldn't see I needed her. It'd happened before.

Sometimes she'll open up, make time, talk, as if it's important, and she cares. Other times she puts on her 'it can't be that bad, let's get down to *real* problems' act – meaning *work*.

I'm proud of what we are, but at the same time I hate it. Wish we were the kind of family that drank real coffee instead of tea and had lots of gadgets in the kitchen. A portable telephone for when we were sunning ourselves in the garden, and didn't want to get up. And we'd *talk*, like they do on the telly.

But I couldn't be like the people on TV. Not really. I pick my nails and I've got quite thin hair, my legs aren't long enough and I don't intend to stretch myself on a rack.

They used to say that marriage was like being stretched on a rack – torture. When an anniversary came they said things like, 'Fifteen years. *Feels like thirty.*'

Then, 'You get less than that for murder.'

Why don't the murderers get all the diseases? A life sentence disease. Then a reprieve, with a re-sentence.

Dad said that things were quiet on the farm, but should soon be back to normal. But when Alex came in looking for a drink, he said we were losing out badly compared to other years. I didn't ask him about it because he'd know that I knew nothing, whereas he knew it all. That wasn't what he wanted to talk about anyway. Reckoned he felt rough, looked all right.

'Typhoid jab,' and he told me all about his forthcoming trip to paradise where it'd be brimming with bare bums and beer. Or so he hoped.

'Eight hundred it's costing. Can't wait. *But you should have seen this needle.* Massive,' gulping a glass of orange, then heading for the door to go and spread the news further. I called after him,

'Prick of the year.'

'You can say that again.'

Dad blamed the boys for the way things were going. I heard him tell Pauline, one of Mum and Dad's friends from the dinner dance days. She'd taken to dropping in,

'Just wanted to make sure you're all right.'

Said she hadn't liked to *impose* before.

She's not like Mum.

Fashionable for a start. Too fashionable. Some of her clothes would suit me better than her. Smart, but a bit too flashy. Always re-touching her make-up and hair. Not really show-offish, but not ordinary either.

'Time on my hands,' she said, 'may as well use it, help you out.'

Her husband didn't mind, said it was a good idea if we needed it. He's out all day and she's bored on her own.

'Had some good times, the four of us,' she remembered.

She brought sweets for Timmy. Magazines for me.

It was funny sometimes, how the two of them could hold completely different conversations with each other, gradually finding common ground.

'Bloody hopeless those boys,' he said, 'don't know their arse from their elbow.'

'She don't look much like you.'

'Who?'

'Francie.'

'The trouble with *them* is, they've got no *experience*, I need somebody who knows the ropes.'

' . . . I s'pose she's got your eyes . . . '

'Mind you, they *think* they know it all.'

' . . . And your colouring.'

'Gone from bad to worse they have, just not interested.'

'Have you thought any more about what I said – you know about a holiday?'

'Holiday? Me business'd be finished by the time I got back.'

'Everybody needs a break.'

'I'll see how it goes. Not that it can get any worse.'

'There you are then. Think about it?'

'I'll think about it.'

Dad said she was 'a good sort'.

Uses the same perfume as Mum. I wished she wouldn't.

I'd said to him that maybe we *could* go on holiday.

'Holiday?! I don't want to go on any bloody holiday. Forget it.'

To start she'd called in about twice a week, but soon it was almost every afternoon. She wasn't pushy, not in an obvious way. Hadn't been invited either, but she seemed genuinely concerned. Mum wouldn't have liked someone in her house, fussing around. So precise.

I should have said,

'Thanks, *but* . . . '

It seemed wrong to turn her help away. And it would have caused another row with Dad. She told me she envied us once, as a family.

Meant it as a compliment.

'I admire your Dad.'

59

I didn't, and maybe that's why her words made me feel uncomfortable.

Anyway, if I couldn't have Mum around the place I didn't want anyone, nobody else was good enough. *She* made the gap bigger, being there but not being Mum.

I needed Mum so much, I wasn't ready to stand on my own two feet.

If I spoke to Dad about anything he'd say,

'Yes,' or,

'No,' or,

'*What now?*'

Or, occasionally,

'That's a stupid question,' or,

'*You would think that.*'

As far as routine went, he'd give orders, make statements, but never consider *my* opinion.

We were together in the same situation, but in separate worlds. How can someone be there, but not be there? How can you live your whole life with someone and only know what they look like, but not what they think or feel? How does it happen?

Pauline was different from us. She kissed people hello and goodbye. I've always wondered what'd be like to be one of those kissing people – always laughed at in our house – called 'budgies', and 'pathetic'. That's why I'd never kiss Mum or Dad goodnight. Mum was really cross once when I put my arms around one of Connie's ponies and kissed it on the nose.

'Thinks more of a mule than she does of us,' she said. 'Wouldn't kiss us if we paid her.'

I used to try. But when somebody makes a fool of you, you don't go back for more. She didn't understand that.

When Robbie phoned I told him I was worried about

Dad.

'Don't be,' he said. 'It's only natural for him to be over-sensitive and depressed. Bound to happen. From what he's told me, he's coping quite well.'

'Sure?' I said.

'He'll be fine. After all, he's a grown man, not a little boy.'

I remember Dad saying once, 'A man that cracks up – he's not a *man*.'

But I know what it's like to feel you're wearing somebody else's head, and I reckon he knew too. So confused that you're a stranger to yourself.

Talking about *heads* isn't allowed. You're bound to get on to 'head-cases', 'nut houses' and 'looney bins'. It's all right to break an arm or a leg. That's straightforward. You fall over, you get it fixed, the end. But it's not all right to be confused.

Pauline cooked sometimes, made us good things. I wouldn't eat them. I was hungry, but I wouldn't eat.

'Don't you like it?'

'No.'

'You should've said, I'd have done something different.'

I ignored her. It smelt so good. But I wouldn't eat it. Dad'd get me on my own,

'Now look . . . '

'Look what?'

'Pauline's a *friend*.'

I didn't mean to make it worse for him. But it was pretty bad for me too. At least *he* had *her*.

Timmy liked her too.

'Pauline always brings me things,' he said.

She said he was gorgeous.

'I'd be pleased if I was you,' Marlene said. 'Means you

don't have so much to do in the house. And it's company for your Dad, you can't blame him . . . '

'You don't understand . . . '

'It's like you're being really, well, *selfish* though.'

'I got to look out for myself. No one else will . . . '

'I didn't think you wanted to be running round after Timmy, wiping his bum every five minutes.'

'Just shut up, Marlene.'

Dad was 'matey' but polite to Pauline. He hadn't treated Mum like that. Sharp, abrupt with her. Never said please or thank you.

Mum wasn't as easy-going as Pauline. She put her foot down over petty things, never important ones. Pauline got more done, had more influence. People knew they could approach her and she wouldn't fly off the handle. She got recognition without having to ask for it. Dad praised her.

'And how's our Fairy Godmother?' he'd say. 'Don't know what we'd do without you.'

'Oh, you'd manage.'

'I don't know . . . don't undersell yourself.'

He never praised Mum. If she knew about Pauline now, I can imagine,

'Does she cook better than me?'

'What does she chat about with Dad?'

'Does she cope better?'

Even though she knew Pauline then, she didn't know her in this situation. She'd be looking for reassurance. Some friend Pauline was, to make Mum feel so anxious and vulnerable. Sitting there, reading to Timmy, as if he was her own. He'd cuddle up. I'd leave them, go round to Connie's.

Find her sitting, usually in the quiet, sometimes in the dark, a vodka bottle on the table, and she'd say something like,

'Y'know what? I looked at it. It looked at me. *No* – I said. And I can't believe I said it. But I did. And I mean it this time.'

She said that just about every week. Then she'd smile, say some piece of wisdom, 'What's the difference between tradition and a bucket of bricks? A bucket.'

We saw quite a bit of her before her kids left, but afterwards she'd had to replace them by doing their chores around the farm herself.

I remember once, ages ago, when we had an old car in one of the fields, how we'd set up an obstacle course and I'd driven her, Mum and Dad round it. Just as we'd got going she decided she needed the loo. I parked in a corner for her to go behind the car and as she did, I drove off. She called us dirty-scheming-shit-bags but we all had a good laugh, including her, stooped there. Knickerless.

Now she kept asking me if I was all right. I'd tell her I was and she'd say, 'Good – 'cos I'm not,' and laugh.

I don't think it was real laughing though.

One night she asked, 'Dad okay I take it?'

Then went down through the list – Timmy, Robbie, Alex, Matt – then – Pauline. As if Pauline was one of us lot. She *must* have noticed I looked surprised.

'How d'you get on with her?'

'She's company for Dad. And she helps out.'

'Um. The little bird that swooped.'

'Saves me doing all the housework.'

'Well, so long as you're happy. That's what counts.'

When I got back home I regretted not telling her the truth.

I just felt I couldn't go on any more, something inside of me, in the place where feelings are stored, screamed.

I cried an explosion. For the first time since Mum had been spirited away.

People shouldn't tell you to calm down, not to cry. They should say – cry, or I'll thump you and make you bloody well cry. Sometimes nothing else will do.

What I want to know is – if God is good, why does He take away the ones we love? Where is He, this God, when a bomb goes off? Or when children are tortured? If He's been around so long, where was He in our history books – when people were being beaten and gassed? Was He down the pub with Hitler – did He have six and a half million pints? I can't find His excuse. Maybe *He's* just an excuse for people who can't do it on their own, who don't want the responsibility. Or was He invented as a way of controlling people, putting the fear of God into them.

I stayed in bed pretty late the next morning. Pauline was there and I didn't want her noticing my puffy eyes – she would have loved to have been credited with that discovery. Always '*glad to be useful*'. I didn't want to do her jobs, didn't want *her* to do them either.

'Came round early today,' she'd said, 'to get a head start on this lot,' nodding towards the washing, piled in the basket. She knew how to work the machine. When Mum died we didn't have a clue.

'You staying all day then?'

'Well, for as long as it takes. Want breakfast?'

'At this time?'

'Breakfast-cum-lunch then.'

'No. I don't really.'

So it was mornings as well as afternoons now.

Dad came in at about one, he'd been off to a sale. Sat in the lounge with tea and their lunch, discussing what he'd bought, how much it'd cost, why it was such a

64

bargain. She agreed with him in all the right places. When they finished, Pauline switched the TV on, kicked off her shoes, lay back in the chair.

'Real nice place you've got here. Cosy.'

Her being at ease made me feel the opposite. Mum worked hard for her home. Now Pauline was the one who was enjoying it.

'She's all right about me, is she?' I heard her ask him, 'You know – she don't mind?'

'She's not a bad kid,' he said, 'I mean she's not like some. Funny age, but she's all right.'

'*But what's she think about me?*'

'She likes you, don't worry, she's level-headed enough.'

She knew how to do things. I wished she was hopeless. Wished she was even better looking, so's I could say, 'She think's she's *it*.'

She asked me out, shopping. I told her I couldn't go because I'd arranged something else. She said we could go another time. I didn't want to, didn't want to like her. If I'd said that, she probably would have told me she understood. I didn't want her to *understand*. I wanted her to feel pushed out, to decide not to bother any more.

I was surprised when I heard their voices coming from the dining room.

'Much better already,' I heard Dad say.

'Haven't started yet . . . '

I watched from the hall as she began to empty the shelves crammed with tatty paperbacks. Picking them up several at a time. Timmy was helping.

'I hate the feel and smell of old books,' she said.

'What shall I put 'em in?' Dad asked her.

'Bin liner'd do . . . if they're going in the attic.'

He turned and saw me. Hesitated.

65

'Cleaning this room up. It's a waste to leave it like this.'

'*They're Mum's books.*'

Couldn't believe it.

'I wasn't doing away with them. Just packing them up.'

Pauline stopped.

'S'pect you might like to have them, would you?'

'I *might* like to leave them where they are. Not that what *I* think counts.'

'Come on Francie,' Dad said, 'you have them then. In your room. That's the best thing . . . '

'I don't want them *in my room*, I want them *here*. *Where my Mum left them.*'

And stomped out.

Walked.

Every step quicker than the last.

Then I ran, to the far side of the paddock. Kicked the fence, the long grass around it. Kicked anything that was in front of me. So much open space, but still that crushed, trapped feeling, pressing down. Why did he want *her* around? She was nowhere near as good as Mum. I stayed down there for an hour or more. When I got back some of the books were re-stacked on the shelf. Some were on my bed. My feelings were jumbled up. I wanted Dad to have friends . . . but not *her*.

She'd come up with different tales, designed to 'cheer me up', 'get me out of myself'.

Told me how once, in church, right in the middle of the Lord's Prayer, the alarm went off on her watch and belted out the James Bond theme tune. I didn't laugh.

She told me how at a job interview she'd tried to act cool and impressive, 'cept when it came to her turn to speak and she'd looked the bloke straight in the eye – to appear confident and forthright – one lens dropped out of her glasses on to her lap. I didn't laugh at that either. Not until she'd gone.

Besides being a comedienne, she was a suggestion machine.

'We could . . . '

'Let's . . . '

'I've got an idea . . . '

My answer was always 'no'.

She said she didn't know much about kids because she'd never had any of her own. She wished she had.

Well, tough. I *wished* I had Mum.

Thought about Mum the whole time. About the things we'd all done together. Like when we went fishing and I fell in, dragging her with me. She didn't worry, it was real funny, we were all covered in slimey weeds and yuk. We had to walk home, people slowed down in their cars to get a closer look at us and we acted as if we always went around like that. Dad said we were 'a right pair', but that he wouldn't change us. Then he presented us with a can of pilchards as a booby prize.

I'd tell Pauline about our good times – to make *her* ideas sound boring in comparison.

'What about this holiday?' she kept saying to Dad.

'Yeah.'

'Yeah what?'

'Yeah, what about it? I'll see.'

I wished he'd just tell her 'no', like he'd told me. Didn't want her to persuade him to do anything that I couldn't get him to do. I told him it was a stupid idea. It would have been nice though – a holiday.

'I'm worried,' she'd said. 'I can't seem to get anywhere with Francie, and it's not that I haven't tried.'

'Yeah,' reading his paper.

'Like, I know it's not easy, but it's so, well . . . '

He didn't answer. I was winning the game when he ignored her.

Even so, some mornings I felt I'd been crying forever, a hundred years. As if there was just no point, not to anything, not to making it to the end of the week. I wanted to stay in bed, never get up again. Never speak to anyone again. Never move. I couldn't shake those feelings off.

Then days would go by and I'd feel all right. Relieved that things were getting better. But the heaviness would come crashing back and knock me down, it was never going to go away for good. When that happened I couldn't imagine being happy again, no matter what.

I'd cry until I had no more energy to spend and could only lie there, wishing. It was overwhelming and frightening.

Mum had said stuff like, 'You'll miss me one day.'

When I'd played up, Dad had said, 'That's another nail in your Mother's coffin.'

Once I said, 'When you're dead I'll be able to do just what I want. *I can't wait.*'

Dying is always a threat. Then when it happens it doesn't seem that it's natural, something that you can be sure is going to happen . . . to them, to you, to everyone.

Can't *buy* your way out of *that.*

Mum was bought. Without him, his money, she imagined she'd be helpless. He kept her, so long as she believed it, so long as she did what he wanted in return, like any job.

In ways it feels as if I should cry for evermore, because if I don't it'd mean that she wasn't important enough. She was. In other ways I feel like I'm insulting

68

her if I can't pick up the pieces, as if she didn't do a very good job with me.

I kept working on, at the farm – but only when they didn't *expect* me to, they had no right to do that.

Matt'd thanked me, said not many people could do a faster job of shit-shovelling, and he was really pleased 'cause it meant he could get off home early. Alex overheard what he said, called him a soft-headed rent-boy,

'Reckon you ought to get her knickers off,' he sneered. He had a girl with him. Seemed to make him walk different than usual, he was striding, like John Wayne.

'Basically,' I heard him say, 'I'm the gaffer around here, up to me buns in work.'

Later on he'd stopped at the house to pick up a letter – all his mail came to us, he didn't want his family opening it and prying.

'They've gone bust,' he said, bewildered. '*The travel company's gone bust!*'

The look on my face must have told all – Dad grabbed me by the shoulder and muttered,

'*Don't* take the mickey.'

So I didn't. Just said how sorry I was, it'd sounded so brilliant, it was a pity that he was going to miss it. And maybe lose all his money.

Me and Pauline had a good laugh about it, she didn't care for him too much either.

She liked to joke, the same as Mum. But when I joined in with Pauline I felt I was letting Mum down. So I mentioned her whenever I could.

'Mum didn't do it like *that*.'

'Mum said . . . '

'Mum was *really* good at . . . '

She'd agree, when I wanted her to disagree.

'I had a lot of time for your Mum.'

'You're always whingeing about Pauline,' Marlene said.

'Wouldn't *you*?'

'She's better than someone like Connie, me Dad reckons she's a tart.'

'*She is not.*'

Silence.

'We always end up arguing lately,' she said.

Went quiet again.

'I know I go on about her. I wouldn't mind so much if I thought she was *just* a friend.'

'What d'you mean? You don't think they . . . *do it* . . . do you?'

'Dunno.'

'But she's *married* and that.'

'I looked in his room . . . to see if I could find anything.'

'They *can't* do. They're too old.'

'Can't imagine it . . . '

'Can't imagine *mine, doing it*. S'pose they must have, at least twice, or me and our Andrew wouldn't be here.'

'Weird thought, innit?'

'Hey, 'member in geography when we hid the store room key in that durex?'

We laughed. Maybe I *was* letting my imagination run away with me. Maybe there wasn't anything like that between them.

Though some people said they thought Dad should have let Mum 'get cold' before he 'dived in' with Pauline. Said, 'Course, it just goes to show.'

Didn't say what it went to show, but I don't s'pose they needed to. Dad said they were talking rubbish, didn't know the facts, and should mind their own business. Pauline didn't say anything except he was entitled to have friends. Some people wouldn't have anything to do with either of them. *I* didn't want it to be true, it was less painful to think them all liars. Pauline's husband said there's no smoke without fire. Told her to go.

'You can't stay *here*,' Dad said.

'You mean . . . It was nothing to you?'

'I mean *you can't stay here*. It wouldn't be right.'

'Just a bit of fun eh? A bit of a laugh at good old Pauline's expense.'

'I'm fond of you, but . . . '

'Yeah – *but* . . . '

'I never set out to split up your marriage.'

'*I* never set out to get led up the garden path.'

'Look . . . '

'Don't waste your breath,' she said, 'I've heard more than enough.'

He said it was best if we didn't 'go on' about 'the Pauline episode' – that it wouldn't 'do any good', and was 'silly really'. It probably was just 'silly really' to him.

A long time ago, Mum was talking, about someone else, 'Who is she?'

'Who?'

'*Her*.'

'Don't know what you're on about.'

'Her. *I'm on about her*.'

'Why d'you do this to yourself?'

'*Tell me. I've got a right to know*.'

'All right, have it your way. Look, it was nothing. She was nothing. Nobody important.'

'Is that what you tell *her* about *me*?'
How can anybody be nobody?

'Keeps asking me if I'm *happy*,' I said to Marlene.
'S'pect he worries about you.'
'It's only since *she's* been off the scene. I'm not here for *his* convenience.'
'He asked me the other day if I knew what you were thinking of doing when we left school. Said he hopes you'll stay around here.'
'He would.'
'I reckon he's scared he'll lose you.'
'Good. I hope he feels rejected – the same way he made me feel.'
'You can't run his life though . . . '
'And *he* can't run *mine*.'
It felt like an atmosphere was gradually cementing me into position, a wall of rocks and ivy, with no hammer heavy enough to bring it to dust. For a while I'd been awarded second prize to somebody else. Then the old feelings came back and I felt swamped by *duty*. But I can't be his mother, or take the place of mine. I wish he hated me. I wish he'd tell me that I had to get out as soon as possible . . . I could beg to stay, he wouldn't hear of it. He'd say I could come back and visit on the days he wasn't too busy.

If he wasn't bothered with me, I wouldn't be capable of hurting him any more than he's hurt already. I wish I hated him too. Be easy then.

Four

We cancelled proper Christmas. I was glad, couldn't have stood the empty space at the table and all around.

'I don't mean to sound horrible,' Marlene said, 'But I told you what I asked them for, right – a ghetto blaster. And what did I get? A bracelet with me name on it. Gold and all that, but I ask you. Talk about naff. Probably fell off the back of a lorry anyway.'

'When you going to your Gran's?'

'This afternoon, till *next Friday*.'

'*Boring*!'

'It'll be *Marlene do this, Marlene do that*. Did I tell you I might change my name? When I'm old enough. It's daft

73

innit – *Marlene*?! After some film star called Marlena'.

'What you gunna change it to then?'

'Dunno. Charlotte, or Chasia . . . '

'*Get off that phone our Marlene*,' a voice shouted from the background.

'Hear that? . . . I can't do *anything* in this house.'

'I'll see you when you get back then.'

'*Marlene* . . . '

'See you soon,' she said.

Pauline came to see Dad, but he said to tell her he was out. She didn't believe it.

'It's all right. I only wanted to wish you a happy Christmas. I'm a bit late I know . . . '

'Thanks.'

'How're you keeping?'

'Okay.'

'We might be moving soon – away. Looking for something up country, something we can do up.'

'That'll be nice.'

'Yeah,' she said.

I told her I was sorry Dad wouldn't see her and that I hoped they found what they wanted. Wondered if I should be ashamed of the way I'd treated her, but figured sometimes you're right, sometimes you're human. Saw her again once when Dad, Robbie, me and Timmy went to see the hunt off. It's a sort of ritual.

I don't like horses much. Or dogs. Or women that wish they were actresses and laugh a lot. Or men that wish they were high court judges and carry whips like perverts. Must make them feel really important, having a crowd turn up to admire them. Who do they think they are?

There were saboteurs too. Dad said *they* were weirdo vegetarians. The spectators laughed at them, the riders

74

ignored them.

I spotted Pauline's husband and moved closer to Dad. He pretended not to notice, blushed a bit, then looked in the opposite direction. I tried to think up some brilliant conversation, then Dad said, 'Look really smart don't they?'

'Yeah,' I said, and caught hold of his arm to make him look like a subdued family man and not an over-sexed one. Pauline's husband was edging his way nearer.

'Isn't that . . . you know . . . over there?' Robbie said, ignorant.

'Who?' Dad said, panic stricken. 'Oh, you mean . . . over there. Yeah, I think it is.'

'What's his name?' Robbie said. 'I've lost it.'

Dad looked sick.

'Haven't seen him for years,' he went on, 'always a good laugh.'

Dad looked sicker. Alex was grinning from the sidelines. I saw he'd changed his image and was now a kind of James Dean character. Dad noticed I'd hooked my arm around his and pulled away. Fine I thought. You'll regret it when he smashes your face in. He went over and spoke to the woman who was scooping up the fresh manure with a shovel, filling herself a bag. I felt nervous for him, unprotected.

'That's my two boys,' he told her, 'and there's Francie, over there look . . . '

'No?!' she said, 'Wouldn't have recognised her . . . '

'They grow up fast these days.'

'Too fast.'

'Think you could be right there.'

'Childhood don't last five minutes any more. They can't wait . . . '

When I had a really good look at Pauline's husband he didn't seem so much of a threat.

Isolated, despite the crowd. Just like Dad.

Everyone was looking at Connie. I think she must have been going for the world record in punch drinking and anything else she could get for free. She flirted with the men, then mouthed 'asshole' and worse, to their backs as they walked off looking smug. She said she didn't agree with fox hunting but was prepared to disagree passively where free booze was involved. Robbie asked her if she could be objectionable in a more passive way, wished he hadn't when she told him she fancied him madly and tried to bite his neck.

After the off, everyone moved inside the pub. There was darts, pool, table skittles and not enough space. Mum would have complained about the noise from the fruit machines and the juke box, and about the condoms for sale in the *ladies* toilet, a pound for three, including two fruit flavours. Timmy was ushered into a room across the hallway, set aside for the younger children.

'Your Mother would have enjoyed a "do" like today,' Dad said.

'She wouldn't.'

'She would've come.'

'Not to enjoy it,' I said, 'but because you'd of kicked up if she hadn't.'

'Christ,' he said, real quiet, 'what's got into you this time?'

'She wouldn't have enjoyed it,' I said, 'you *know* she wouldn't. She would have come because it was easier than *not* coming.'

'Look, I was only saying . . .'

'Well don't because it's not true.'

People looked at us. He sank into his chair. I felt

guilty.

'There's not enough time to go falling out with each other,' Connie said. 'The last time I done any falling out was when I wore a padded bra that was too small.'

Ha ha. People were getting fed up with her, giving a snigger at best. I didn't like her like this.

Then, Dad said to me,

'Any why did *you* come?'

'What?'

'You heard. Why did *you* come?'

'I dunno. Because you made me I s'pose.'

'*Made you*?! I never said anything.'

'You didn't have to.'

'What am I? Bloody subhuman with special powers or something? I don't know what your Mother'd think of you carrying on like this.'

'Ding ding,' Connie said, 'end of second round.'

Robbie told us to shut up and we did.

Seemed a long time since me and Robbie'd had our contests – who could stay up the latest, who could stay in bed the latest, who could go longest without talking.

Our beefburger and chips came, mine was coldish but I didn't dare say so. I got on with it, looking at the photos on the wall, the cricket teams, the five-a-side teams, the darts teams and a guide dog called Sally, paid for by the patrons. The woman from the post office told me to cheer up. She can talk, I reckon being miserable's a vital qualification to get work with the Post Office.

After eating we went back outside because the sun was shining and it was 'a beautiful day'. Don't worry about the frost-bite, savour the surroundings. They all *looked*. I didn't know what we were supposed to find so magical in a few trees and fields and a bit of blue sky. I mean, so what? Doesn't say much to me. It's boring.

They were all going, 'Ahhh . . . ' like you feel you have to when somebody pushes their new baby at you.

Ahhh . . . what?

I tried to wind them up by saying the wasted space should be used to build blocks of flats, but they were too appalled to answer. Dad gave me his gloves and I assumed all was forgiven.

He was speaking to some people he knew,

' . . . can't make out what happened to the *old crowd*. Was a time when they were *always* about, s'pose they're settled now, don't go in for *pubbing*, not like they used to. Don't like to ring them up. But the youngsters aren't as easy to mix with. A different generation, not like the old days.'

He reminded me how once I'd nicked some empty bottles from the pub yard and taken them in to claim the deposit back. But I hadn't seen 'Weedkiller – do not drink' scrawled all over them *in the landlady's handwriting*. She wasn't impressed.

'Little sod,' Dad said, 'I could've knocked your block off.'

Then, 'Remember when we used to come down here, the four of us – before we had Timmy?'

We used to sit in the passageway because kids weren't allowed in the bars. We had cherry drinks, crisps, pickled eggs, chocolate. It was good.

'Sunday nights,' I said.

The wicker chairs used to scratch my legs and the cats used to leave their hairs all over my clothes. I used to boast to other kids that I'd 'been in the pub until late'. I don't know why now, judging what it did for Connie.

Timmy was playing with a group of kids. When I

78

saw one of the little ones grab her Mum and Dad's hands and swing between the two it made me feel funny, I used to do that.

Dad was watching the other people, the families. Suddenly said, 'It was a good marriage.'

I thought of them, at opposite ends of the house.

'Got on well together,' he said.

I thought of all their silences.

'I mean, everyone has their ups and downs . . . '

I thought of their fighting.

'*But it was a good marriage.*'

In my head I heard him saying to her, 'You haven't *put on a few pounds* – you've *let yourself go.* Other women keep themselves together, why can't you?'

'She was a trouper,' he said, 'always coped, always managed.'

He went on, proud, 'If ever I brought people back home, no matter how late, she'd always get out of bed, look after things, be sociable. She was good like that. The best.'

I didn't answer.

'Nothing would have parted me from your Mother and you kids.'

He was right, it wouldn't have done. She held it together too well. She did too much.

I caught sight of Pauline. Dad said it was time to go. So I took Timmy home, but he went to Connie's with a couple of others. An hour or so went by then he came in. Sat down. Looked at me in the way I don't like.

'Know what I felt when I realised she was dying? I thought – I don't care how much she has to suffer, I can't let her die. Is that terrible? Then, when it happened, I just felt lost, completely lost. And guilty. Didn't know what to do. I'd do anything to bring her back. I would.'

He carried on, 'I can't help thinking, how we should-'ve . . . I don't know . . . She deserved different . . . You wouldn't understand.'

'Try me.'

'No. I'm drunk. I've said enough.'

He put his hand on my head. It made me shiver.

'I always done what I thought was best. It might not have been, but you do what seems right at the time.'

He moved his hand away.

'Still. You'll be here. That's some consolation.'

Said he was going to sleep off the drink.

'Don't let on to Robbie that I've had one too many when he gets in.'

A day or so later when I'd gone round to Connie's she was at the vodka again. She slid the bottle behind the curtain, out of sight, but she knew I'd seen.

'Too late for me to change now,' and she hid behind her smile.

'Think so?'

Her smile faded.

'So it's an excuse,' she said, 'a cop out.'

I sat down next to her.

'What about you,' she said. 'Things all right?'

She didn't look surprised when I said no.

'At least you can admit it. I never could.'

'What stopped you?'

'Reasons.'

She sounded bitter.

'I don't know. I s'pose I expected to be put down and so I took it.'

'So did Mum.'

'Daresay she had her reasons too.'

She lit a cigarette.

'Whatever you do,' she said, 'don't give in.'

I've felt like giving in sometimes. But I don't want to end up like Connie. Or like Mum. Don't want to be as selfish as I am either. I'm *trying* to make decisions.

'You're *late*,' Marlene said.

'I know, sorry, been round Connie's.'

'You're *always* round there.'

'I'm *not*. But so what if I was?'

'I've been waiting for you.'

'We're not *going* anywhere are we?'

'No.'

'Well then . . . '

She wouldn't let it drop.

'Dunno why you bothered to come, you'll have to go soon.'

'What's got into you? I went to Connie's first – *big deal*.'

She sat there picking at her jumper, rolling the fluff between her fingers.

'What shall we do then?' I said.

She shrugged.

'Don't care.'

'I'll go now if you want.'

'Please yourself.'

'Look, what's wrong with you?'

'Nothing.'

'There *is*.'

'Nothing I can't handle.'

'*Tell me*!'

'*No*.'

I turned to go.

'It's me Dad,' she said.

'What about him?'

'The court case. It's next week.'

81

'Oh . . .'

She stood up, walked over to the window.

'Solicitor reckons he'll go down this time.'

'Go *inside*?'

She nodded.

'How come? It wasn't *that much* money, was it?'

'He didn't tell us the whole story. There was more to it than we thought.'

'He lied about it . . . ?'

'*He only wanted to protect us.*'

'How much was it then?'

'Not sure. But he's been done before hasn't he. He just never meant it to go this far.'

'Knew what he was doing though didn't he?'

'No. Well, yeah. Oh, I dunno. Leave it. Forget I said anything.'

'It's true though, why should you . . .'

'*He's all right, me Dad. Just leave me alone if you're gunna be like that.*'

She went and sat back on her bed, hugged her knees close to her body, buried her head.

'Sorry.'

She didn't answer.

'How long d' they think he'll get?'

'*I dunno*,' she snapped. Then said softly, 'what about me Mum?'

'What's she said about it?'

'Nothing much. Keeps crying.'

'She'll get by somehow.'

'It'd be awful to think of him, in there. I couldn't bear it.'

She paused.

'We wanted nice things see. Kept on, me as well, not just me Mum.'

'It's not your fault, you didn't make him do it.'

'Didn't make him, but he was doing it for us. I probably helped.'

'*You didn't.*'

She got angry again,

'*I could kill him sometimes.*'

'It might not turn out as bad as you think. He might get off yet.'

'Have to see. Don't sound too good though does it? I'm dreading next Wednesday. Me sodding birthday as well – just my luck.'

I heard her Dad come in downstairs.

'I'm so ashamed,' her Mum shouted.

'So you keep saying,' he said, 'now just *shut it.*'

Their arguing went on, 'You're only thinking of yourself,' he told her, 'what about *me?*'

Doors banged, then I heard him start up his car again, drive off.

'I'll never forget me sixteenth will I?' Marlene said.

'Would have been Mum's birthday soon.'

'She was good, your Mum.'

'I never even bought her a present last year. Spent the money on a new shirt. I was gunna buy her something nice, something she'd really like. Never got round to it. Keep thinking about that.'

'You got on well though.'

'Not really.'

'You *did.*'

'Well, not too bad I s'pose.'

'She was dead funny sometimes.'

'Yeah. S'pose she was. 'Member when she had a *little chat* with you for swearing?'

'*Do I!*'

'I was *so* embarrassed . . . tried to get my own back

83

for you later . . . told her she looked like a demented chicken in her new high heel shoes . . . '

' . . . and she turned round and squirted us with washing-up liquid.'

'It was *everywhere* . . . '

'I know . . . in our hair, all over our jeans . . . '

'She was well pleased with herself . . . '

'We all cracked up . . . '

'What about when we stuck those transfers on our arms . . . told her we'd had tattoos done in town . . . *her face*!!!'

But Marlene's smile didn't last.

' . . . Don't know why we're laughing. Not much to look forward to is there?'

I tried to think of something.

'There's always the South of France . . . '

Also by Sandra Chick
Push Me, Pull Me

Cathy is fourteen and lives with her Mum. Then Bob,
Mum's new boyfriend moves in and everything changes.
Mum seems to care about nothing but pleasing him all
the time and she often gets angry with Cathy.

Then Cathy's world falls apart. Bob rapes her and she
doesn't know where to turn for help. She just can't cope
anymore and starts to act up at school, even losing her
best friend Sophie.

Slowly, very slowly, her anger surfaces and Cathy begins
to work it all out.

ISBN: 0 7043 4901 9
Fiction   £2.95

Maude Casey
Over the Water
Shortlisted for the Whitbread Literature Award. A
moving novel about an Irish girl growing up in England,
and an eventful summer holiday 'back home'.
0 70043 4905 1   £2.95

Ann Considine and Robyn Slovo, editors
Dead Proud
Playscripts from Second Wave Young Women
Playwrights. About shoplifting, getting pregnant,
mothers and other difficulties.
0 7043 4908 6   £2.95

Jeni Couzyn, editor
Singing Down the Bones
A lively collection of poetry about feeling 'special',
having a mission in life, being ready to change the world
– all the natural optimism of the teenage girl.
0 7043 4913 2   £3.50

Jill Dawson, editor
School Tales
Some daring tales told out of school, by 17 young writers
(all under 25).
0 7043 4922 1   £3.50

Christina Dunhill, editor
A Girl's Best Friend
Fourteen stories about friendship and jealousy, and all
the feelings in between. A Selected Title for Children's
Book Week 1988.
0 7043 4907 8   £2.95

Gwyneth Jones
The Hidden Ones
A brilliantly written novel about Adele, a computer
games whizz-kid with strange powers.
0 7043 4910 8   £3.50

Norma Klein
Older Men
Exciting novel about problem fathers by well known and
popular author of many teenage books.
0 7043 4128 X   £3.50

Angela Martin
You Worry Me Tracy, You Really Do
Crackling cartoons on teenage problems such as fat
thighs, parents and 'how far to go'.
0 7043 4902 7   £2.95

Melisa Michaels
Skirmish
Science fiction without macho heroes, about Melach
Rendell, Skyrider.
0 7043 4906 X   £3.50

Kate Murphy
Firsts: British Women Achievers
Scientists, pirates, motor-racing drivers…the first in their
field, placed in history at last.
0 7043 4917 5   £3.50

Millie Murray
Kiesha

A pacey story about a thirteen year-old Black girl born in London with Jamaican parents and a passion for Michael Jackson.

0 7043 4129 8   £2.95

Eileen Fairweather
French Letters

The Life and Loves of Miss Maxine Harrison, Form 4a. A hilarious series of letters between Maxine and her best friend. Hailed as a girls' *Adrian Mole.*

0 7043 4903 5   £2.95

Patricia Grace
Mutuwhenua
The Moon Sleeps

An exciting romance about contrasting values – old and new, Maori and Pakeha – set in contemporary New Zealand.

0 7043 4911 6   £2.95

Jean Holkner
**Aunt Becky's Wedding
and other traumas**
Fourteen tantalising stories about Jewish family life,
featuring Mr Krapinsky the 'Kosher Killer', 'Market Maisie'
and Aunt Becky who finally makes it to the synagogue.
0 7043 4915 9   £2.95

Kristin Hunter
The Soul Brothers and Sister Lou
Reissue of a 1960s cult novel about inner-city kids.
Winner of the Council on Inter-racial Books for Children
prize, and a 'Selected Twenty' title for Feminist Book
Fortnight 1987.
0 7043 4900 0   £3.50

Millie Murray
**Lady A —
a teenage DJ**
A lonely teenager gains confidence when she takes a job
on a local community radio station.
0 7043 4920 5   £2.95